Society
of
Lost Causes

Ophelia Finsen

Also by Ophelia Finsen

Lovers of Old Films
This is Living

Published using Lulu.com
ISBN 978-0-9559923-3-9

The Society of Lost Causes
2007: First Quarterly

All members were present. The following was agreed:

1. Mrs Bridget Driscoll has been as much of a success as could be hoped. She ought to be removed now.

2. Current investigations into Mr Jonathon Martin have been more successful than originally anticipated. Everyone is particularly pleased with the in depth report collaborated on. The end product will now be made public.

3. The society's next subject will be Miss Saskia Weaver. The society has very little information on which to start investigations, but it was agreed that this subject has been neglected by the society's attention for too long. Work will commence immediately.

When polished rose quartz looks like milk-pink wisps of breath caught up in ice. It is easy to understand why the spiritualists claim the rock contains properties of love, forgiveness and energy. Geologically speaking, it is a member of a larger family of minerals, going under the common name of quartz, or *crystalline silica*. There was a local source somewhere; shards appearing in the river, or so they said. It had been suggested that there was a tract in the ground beneath the folly, but that was more a conclusion of local lore than any scientific investigation.

The woman stood mid-calf-deep in the river. She arched her back and held the small, chipped stone up to the fading light. The twists of colour were barely visible. Dusk had arrived. She tossed the stone into a plastic container on the river bank.

She knew she would look deranged, eccentric at the very least to passers by. Even if she had cared, the damage would be minimal. It was a chilly Sunday night, the light going, and few people ventured into the park. They had better pursuits to engage in.

Her dress skirts hitched up around her thighs, black hair tied scruffily on the back of her head to keep it out of the water. Hands on hips she looked down at the round sieve, submerged on an angle at her feet. River grit and pebbles at the bottom. It was pointless panning for stones anymore. The light had gone and she wouldn't tell the difference between precious metals and minerals from bashed cement clumps and congealed dirt.

She reached into the shallow river with both hands, pulling the weight of the sieve up. She watched with a child-like fascination as the water poured out when it broke the surface. Turning it over, she shook the rejects back into the river. Small pebbles splashed into the water.

She was leaning forward, washing out the sieve when she heard the pounding footsteps. She glanced up between locks of tousled hair to the path that wound through the forest. On nearing the shallow crossing point over the stream, it split off – one track up the hill to the folly, the other out over the green. She jolted straight as the jogger – a tall man in shorts and a sweat-stained t shirt, bounded out from the trees. Water splashed down her dress. She clutched the sieve like a weapon. The jogger was disconnected from the peace of the evening, plugged into a MP3 player, music roaring in his ears. He stopped running when he saw her, staring quizzically at the oddity in the river. He pulled one of the earplugs out.

Staring at her like she was a freak. Her face set in a scowl in response, she marched out of the river, picking up her bags in a haughty manner. Like the guilty trying to cover over a secret. He opened his mouth to say something, almost ready to apologise but not sure what for. The stranger had already slipped into her sandals and was charging out across the green, her image dispersing with the fuzzy light.

He glanced to the path up to the folly. He had intended to run up there for the extra exertion, but the woman's angry stare had set him off balance. He couldn't think what he had done wrong. Shrugging to himself, he stuck the plug back into his ear and jogged out onto the green. An early night this time.

Further up into town a man stood on a ladder propped up against a street lamp. He had a coil of thick wire slung over one shoulder, worn fingers fumbling with the end. Trying to twist it onto a home-made construction attached to the top of the lamp. Something tapped on the brim of his hat, and he looked up into the darkening sky. The first drop of evening rain. Very fitting that he should be the one to catch it.

Cursing as the wire nicked one of his fingers, he looked back down at the task in hand. He should have remembered the pliers, but had left them somewhere in the shop. Fixing a display after the doors were locked.

He raised his head slightly, staring down the quiet residential street and the line of dormant parked cars, searching for a figure who was not there. Damn that boy; he was always roaming.

He put his finger in his mouth to staunch the blood.

The boy appeared around the corner, back from his errand. He raised the object he had been sent to collect, like a salute to the man on the ladder. The boy was a spotty little urchin, nothing immediately apparent to endear him to anyone. Probably why his parents did not bother, barely noticing that he was alive. And the old man had taken pity. Besides, he had never had an assistant before who had taken such an interest in his experiments.

He started to walk forward, then halted, uncertain, almost sniffing the air for danger. There was something almost rat like about him, the man reflected. He saw something and bolted back around the corner out of sight. Now what?

"Now then, Mr Wagstaff."

The voice was very recognisable. It explained why the boy had fled. The old man closed his eyes, resting his forehead against the lamppost. Dear Lord, give me strength. He guessed one of the nosey residents - little mind, petty lifestyle - had been watching from behind a corner of curtain and had rung to complain. Not even knowing what it was that could possibly grieve them.

"Are you playing deaf now?" the voice persisted.

The man released an audible sigh. "It's Professor," he corrected, twisting round to glance down on the police constable. Sam Seger. Already an obnoxious little runt back in the days of shorts, lollipops and pea shooters. Even then he was always marching along, telling the other boys what to do. One of those irritating youths who were born believing they knew best, that people of another generation simply didn't understand the way the world worked.

The young P.C. smirked to himself. They all knew the Professor's credentials were real – he'd checked himself a couple of years ago in an unsuccessful bid to show the old man up - but it was hard to image that long-haired, grey-haired lunatic as a person of any authority. Just a small time businessman trying to make life interesting. As if anyone cared about his experiments. "I seem to remember I've already had this conversation with you. And you're still too old to be shimmying up lampposts, don't you think?"

Patronising little sod; he was only sixty. Giving the end of the wire a tug to suggest he was detaching the only thing he'd put up there, the Professor Wagstaff climbed down the ladder. The metal frame work groaned under each step.

"You need authorisation from the council to deface their property," Seger spoke to him as if he didn't speak English.

"I was just going to conduct a weather experiment," he replied calmly. "Don't you have any real criminals to catch?"

The policeman sniffed the air. "You know as well as I do, our crime rate is low. Just a case of keeping the trash under check."

'The trash': dear god. And this was supposed to be the age of political correctness gone mad.

"Better pack it up," P.C. Sam Seger nodded to the ladder. "I'll help you carry it back to your car."

"So gracious of you," the Professor gave a sarcastic little bow. As he turned to click the supports off and drop the top half of the ladder, he gave the light fitting a quick glance. Unless you really looked closely, you wouldn't notice it was there. He'd be back.

"Serving boy not with you tonight?"

"If you're referring to Alan, no, he's not." He must have ducked out of sight before Sam Seger had seen him. Sam did have the type of mind that could only focus on one thing at a time though. He would have seen the Professor at the top of the ladder and blanked the rest of the street out.

"Is he still working at the quarry?" Sam asked casually as he picked up the end of the ladders. A couple of meters between them, they swung around in the street and started back up towards his car. Sam would have undoubtedly already found it. He had the number plate inscribed in the back of his notepad. Good old plod.

"Yes. He'll soon have been there a year."

Sam smirked again. "Well, it doesn't require a lot of thinking, does it? Better than being a delinquent though. How old is he, now?"

"Nineteen," he begrudgingly answered the question, thankful his car was only parked around the corner. He had been planning on going up to the folly to fix some measuring instruments of his own design, but having been caught by Seger this early on in the proceedings, it would have to wait until another night.

The folly was on the peak of a wooded hill at the edge of the park, overlooking the market town. A stone construction with no earthly means of getting into or onto it. There was a good view of the surrounding area from the base in winter when the trees had lost their leaves. A point of interest. Soon to become a very different kind of point of interest for the locals.

Tuesday morning found Jack Dougan sat on the staffroom windowsill gazing out onto the grey street. Pedestrians lugging shopping bags, cars crawling down the road. A dog tied to a lamppost outside the off-license yapping, terrified it was going to be forgotten.

He turned his back on the town and lifted the cog up to his eye. He examined the section of metal, unaware of the oil smears on his fingers. He was ninety percent sure this was the offending cog, the one that was rattling and groaning after five minutes of running. Normally a little noise in any machine would not be an issue, but this was loud enough to be audible in the back seats, a sound like a phantom couple reliving an old rendez vous. It had been well oiled when he had taken it out of the projector, which cancelled out his immediate presumption. Still, it gave him something to do.

The door to the shabby staff room opened. Jack only gave it a cursory glance. Amanda Turner, in pristine business suit and garish pink lipstick, hand bag with newspaper sticking out, walked in with a scowl on her face. She brightened when she saw Jack quietly brooding in the corner.

"You're in very early," she commented as she flicked the kettle on to boil. "In fact, by my calculations, three hours too early. Tuesday matinee for the pensioners doesn't start till three."

"Yeah, well, the projector was rattling on Sunday. Thought I'd come in and take a look before the next show."

Amanda savoured the sound of his voice for a moment before replying. Jack and his family had moved back to the north of England when he was eleven, but even now there was that slightest hint of an Australian accent underneath the northern vowels. He'd been the perk of the job that had clinched her accepting the offer of cinema manager two years ago. Tall, sweeping loose brown hair; warm, beautiful eyes; broad shoulders; in good shape; she had watched him from a distance whilst the previous manager, a short egg-featured man had bleated about standing in the community. She had visions of passionate meetings across her desk. Accidental bumps in the darkened auditorium. Marriage within the year. Reality wasn't quite the fantasy. To date she hadn't had anything more than a friendly hug.

"Not that it really matters," he continued thoughtfully, "They're all as deaf as coots, the Tuesday bunch."

He laughed and she had to turn away to the cupboard so that he wouldn't see her rather pathetic grin. "Can I get you a cup of tea?"

"No, I'm all right."

"Amanda?" The postman's bawdy voice roared up the staircase before him. "You about?"

There was a sharp clink as she set the mug down. Terry.

Terry was a red faced, round, meaty man who looked like he enjoyed a pint or two and a kick about with his mates. His short cropped blond hair made him look like he was balding. Little eyes pushed like buttons into plasticine. Cocky character, very friendly. Very desperate for a woman. The woman. He never just put the letters through the post box. Always had to deliver them personally into Amanda's hands. Jack watched in amusement as Terry gazed at Amanda like a hungry dog.

"You two up here gossiping?" he asked, his thick, gruff Yorkshire dialect dropping letters and emphasising glottal stops.

"We're cinema folk," Jack joked. "We're too cultured for gossip."

"Oh ay," Terry raised his eyebrows, watching Amanda stir her tea. "But this is gossip for everyone. Even you folks couldn't resist a good murder."

"Murder?" Jack was laughing, not taking him seriously.

Terry was going to be here all day if Jack got him going. It was too early in the week for this. "Is that the post?" Amanda asked curtly, pretending not to be interested in the drama she was desperate to hear about.

"That's your post." Terry handed it across.

"Right, thanks, Terry," she said cheerily, turning away to sit down at the table. Pretending to sort the post. Hoping he'd take the hint.

"Well, I'd better be off," Terry said, looking uncertainly from Amanda to Jack. Suddenly self- conscious, he backed out of the room and thundered down the staircase.

"See you later," Jack called after him. He waited a moment, looking over at Amanda who was shuffling the post like a pack of cards. "I think you're breaking his heart."

"Oh, don't be ridiculous," she snapped. "There are more important things to think about." She lent across and picked up her handbag. "Like who was murdered."

"I think he was joking."

"I don't." She took the paper from her bag and spread it out on the table top.

Jack stared down at the headlines. "He wasn't."

Amanda almost took a jolt back from the table. A murder had happened here? This was just a little rural town. There were pub brawls now and then, lost walkers, bored youths vandalising property, but murder was not commonplace. She stared at the pictures, familiar places. Scanning over the information already released to the press.

"What's happened?" Jack pressed for details, walking around the table to get a look at the paper.

"Some guy found a body up by the folly yesterday morning. They think he was killed sometime Sunday evening." She put her hand up to her mouth. "His throat was cut. They have no idea who did it. There's some maniac roaming about."

"I doubt it," Jack muttered, turning the paper slightly to get a better look at the photo, leaving fingerprints on the side of the sheet. "It doesn't mention who was killed. Christ, they say here he died in the early evening. I was out running round there then."

Amanda looked horrified. "But that could have been you."

"I'm sure this guy's been upsetting someone. Most murders make very dull film fodder."

She was not convinced by his laid back attitude – although this was the way Jack approached most things in life. She looked back at the article. "It says at the end anyone in the park Sunday evening should contact the police. You should call them."

Jack read the telephone number for the incident room. "Yeah, I suppose I should."

"The point is, I really think you should have taken some photos yourself."

Grumbling on the other end of the line.

"I'm not asking for works of art. This is the digital age..." Laughter. "Yeah, I know. I know. There are some fantastic photographs, but if we use one of those we get into copyright, fees and all kinds of crap and hassle... yeah, exactly."

More talk.

Jack raised his eyes to the ceiling and wished Crispin would admit defeat and end the telephone call. Underneath the protests, the only issue the man was really having was how much petrol he would have to burn to take another trip back to the ship. Money, money, money. Where was the passion these days? Leaning back in his chair, pushing the back rest as far as it would go, he dumped his feet on the desk and started to stretch out the telephone cord. He looked back to the flickering computer screen. His big feet in front. He had a hole in one of his socks. Funny he'd never noticed it this morning.

"So what do you think?"

Jack blinked, for a moment wondering who he was talking to. "Yeah, yeah. I see your point," he bluffed, unaware of what Crispin had been digging for. It didn't matter really, he wouldn't get his way. "But the real issue here is that we are a specialist publication with a limited output. We're never going to have the funds to go crazy. Not that I'm saying money is important." He held up his hands – pointless considering Crispin couldn't see him, being sat in a leaking cottage in Cornwall – hearing another protest growing in the man's throat. "If the world ran according to me, we wouldn't even worry about things like that. But since Simon buggered off in his longboat, I've been left in sole charge of the pennies."

"You're being a tight-arse."

He laughed loudly at that comment. Takes one to know one. "I know, but it's the way it's gotta be." He leaned forward, feet still on the table, a quick stomach crunch to snatch at a bundle of paperclipped sheets. "Look, the article is pretty much there now. Couple of tiny adjustments - I'll email them to you later tonight. It's really just the photography I'm hankering after." He paused. "You do realise you'll get a separate fee for the photos?"

Thoughtful pause. "All right," the disembodied voice relented. "I'll see what I can do this weekend."

"Excellent," Jack beamed. "Get them emailed to me a.s.a.p. I want this in the next issue. See you."

He hung up before Crispin could ask how much his fee was going to be. Jesus, the man was a pain. How had Simon coped with all of this? Little wonder he had decided to attempt a Norway to Canada crossing in a longboat with a gang of pumped up Norwegians and a pierced Icelander with too much free time in charge. Mad, the lot of them, absolutely mad.

Still, it was increasing their subscriptions internationally, and they'd all been hit by the sailing bug at one time or another. Jack tossed Crispin's article in the general direction of the computer and closed his eyes. Summoning up the sound of the sea. That summer sailing on a tea clipper. He'd really worked hard at the rowing before then, to get into shape. Extremely necessary considering the size of him prior. He'd never been a monster, but certainly a portly gent with too much of a liking for mashed potato and the sweet things in life. That had been over three years ago, and since he had been very careful not to let his new found standard drop. Not that he was an overly vain man – no more than any other male at least – but he had really noticed the benefits in so many aspects of his life, and not just the plummet in clothes size.

On the screen was an article by Marian the archaeologist. Well-researched, fascinating (as always) but the woman did not appreciate the complexities of the grammar of her native tongue for someone who was making a living out of writing. He really needed to go through and gut the thing to get coherent sense, but it had been a long day. Too much for this tired editor to continue today.

Switching off the computer, he left the head office of *Naval and Seafaring History* (a converted master bedroom) and tramped down the stairs to the kitchen for a beer. Passing by that photograph on the wall of Shane's graduation – MSc in Engineering – 18 years ago. Jack, a chubby and awkward sixteen year old stood by his mother and gazing admiringly up at his athletic older brother. Jack paused, examining his previous self. He looked like another person. He tapped the glass as if to wake the teenager up. "Weren't a hit with the girls, were you, mate?"

He wasn't either when he'd first moved to the town; quiet, studious, overweight, and having just tumbled into the passenger seat for the magazine, co-driving with Simon. It had been a noticeable addition to his earnings from freelance proofreading.

Something that was a little more engaging and allowed for his own input as well.

The periodical had a wide net of staff scattered across the world (mainly Europe), in touch by telephone and email but rarely face-to-face. Locked away in his home, one job he loved, another he could not complain about; but the solitude was enough to drive anyone mad. He'd taken going to the cinema a lot, fallen in talking with the projectionist (an eighty year old with a penchant for fast vintage cars). The old man had taught him everything about the cinema for two years before wrapping his latest acquisition around a well-established oak. The tree still stands, the car was eventually sold off to another enthusiast near London and the old man, tragically passed away. Immediately dead, a smile on his lips, blood on his face and a fading glint in his eyes. It had been a forgone conclusion that Jack would take over the part-time job of projectionist in the run-down, but charismatic local cinema.

It was around that time that he'd started to loose the weight. The fragility of it all had kicked something in his subconscious. Exercise, diet, no you've had enough mash now. A year later he was doing a lot better and looking forward to the long summer trip sailing on the tea clipper. He got back, and suddenly the town that had known him for three years was looking at him in fresh light. At least the women were.

With all that sudden female attention, he had gone a bit mad at the beginning. Never in on an evening. Lots of girlfriends. A lot of fun. Some control he'd managed to keep – drawing the line at anyone married, and his boss, Amanda, who had made puppy eyes at him the moment she'd come for her first interview.

Nothing had lasted particularly long and he'd grown tired of beginnings that would never develop to full plots. Never a prude, the meaningless sex had been very enjoyable, but the girls had always been hoping for the long term. What went wrong? The old adage proved true. Beauty is only skin deep. And whilst that lean body and Ozzie good looks had reeled them in, as they got to know the man underneath – one who had never changed despite the body transformation – they realised that they couldn't sign up for a life with this much eccentricity.

Boats. Jack liked them. A lot. Boats, ships, warships, longboats, clippers, fleets… He liked to read books about them. Edit a magazine about them. Sail on them. Visit them. Perhaps if it had ended there, a couple of girls might have relented and said 'oh, all right, you'll do. I suppose I could marry you' (not that he'd ever asked). It was the models that got them every time.

When they realised the truth about that high shelf going right around the living room was packed with the most impressive of his creations. That he bought detailed plans of historic ships and vessels so that his models would be just right, exactly to scale and without a bloody piece of rigging out of place. That little boy had never grown up. Winning the lottery fantasies consisted of buying a swimming pool and re-enacting great naval battles. People from the publication could come over and help. It would be brilliant. Nothing he'd ever admitted to anyone – certainly not suitable bedroom talk when women wanted to share secrets. But they saw it there in his eyes, maybe not realising what it actually was, but a gut sensation telling them it really wasn't going to work out.

Jack sighed, beer in hand, as he sat down at the kitchen table. The contents of his jacket pocket had been tossed on the top along with the unopened electricity bill he'd picked up when he'd finally landed home. Keys, loose change, a credit card and a business card from the police. Setting the beer down, his closed his eyes. Three hours at the police and he hadn't even done anything. Sam Seger was a pillock.

Amanda had eventually persuaded him to go to the police after rereading the news article about the recent murder up at the folly. She'd started to look a bit panicky. Got to get that killer caught and locked up before he slaughters the lot of us. The police need your help, Jack.

In the grand schemes of investigations, there had been very little he had been able to tell them. He'd been out jogging that Sunday evening, and had indeed been in the park. He'd considered running up to the folly, it was something he often did. Really got the heart pumping, great for stamina building. Sam had raised an eyebrow - a move he'd probably picked up off daytime detective series. But you didn't that evening. No, I didn't. Why not?

Fair question. Why hadn't he? He'd run through his mental images of the evening and stopped at the stream. There had been a stranger stood in the middle of the river. In the dimming light, she had looked as though she had been panning for gold. No gold in these parts. He must have startled her, because she had given him such an offended stare before marching off.

"Marching off to the folly?"

"No, she'd headed out over the park."

"But she'd been there."

"Doesn't really mean anything, though, does it?"

Sam had never answered that question. He'd scribbled something down, then turned the sheet over so that Jack couldn't read it. He'd asked for a description. Jack had stepped back into the dusky evening, repeated running down the track towards the stream. Startled her again. She was vaguely familiar – which wasn't saying much considering he'd lived here six years now and it wasn't that big a town. He'd most probably seen her walking down the high street. Certainly didn't know her personally. But the description seemed to mean something to Seger; the more Jack said, the more the man nodded and said he thought he knew who Jack was talking about. But he wouldn't tell him her name, just as he wouldn't tell Jack anything about the murder.

Jack took a sip of his beer and mulled over the sparse details the paper had offered this morning. Most probably it was two people settling a score away from prying eyes. An argument that had become a little too heated. Even so, it had been a relatively violent, nasty murder. You could understand that edgy look Amanda had carried with her the rest of the day. If it had been random, just some nutter out for a walk with his knife, then anyone might be next.

If he'd been a dramatic worrier, he might have considered a gym membership over running outdoors, but Jack could never be bothered going down that road. He went back upstairs to change into his jogging clothes. A quick run before bed was just the thing he needed.

The Professor Hammond Wagstaff sat with a cup of tea and wondered to himself if she had always been like this. He watched Dionne stuff chocolate digestive biscuits into her mouth. She was already on her second cup of tea, gulping it down as if she would have to run for a bus before the next minute was over. She always had her tea milky. Said she needed the calcium.

She finished the drink and glanced over at the kettle. He watched her, bemused. "We've another ten minutes till we open; you have time for another cup."

She grinned at him, before scampering back up to the kettle. "I don't know what's wrong with me. I'm so hungry. And so tired."

I wonder too, Wagstaff mused silently. Reflecting on the three years she had worked here, he noted that she had not always been this way. The first year there had never been any odd behaviour. Odd being such a relative word, but nothing that would make him worry. Sometime during the second year she had changed. Subdued almost. Very keenly aware of food. Nothing was ever forgotten in the staff room after that. Of course, this being Dionne, he knew better than to ask.

So she sat there in the scruffy armchair, looking like Egypt's answer to Bridget Bardot – although she had connection to neither France nor North Africa – and longing to a place or time she couldn't get to. She was chasing a teabag around in the hot water with a teaspoon. Eyes expertly lined in dark kohl downcast, copper shimmer on the lids. Satisfied it was strong enough, she twisted in her seat and catapulted the tea bag in the direction of the sink. It hit the tiling on the wall and slid down onto the stainless steel panelling. Settling back into the familiar chair, she stretched her booted legs out in front. "I saw a television crew on my way in this morning."

"Must have been reading the local rags yesterday."

"Yeah," she laughed dryly. "What can we fill the half hour with? Still, a mysterious, bloody murder is something a bit different for this area. Really put us on the map."

"Good to see you haven't lost that compassionate streak," he commented lightly. "But I doubt it will be sensational enough to have any lasting impression on the local consciousness. You know as well as I do that the majority of murders are committed for the most mundane of reasons. It was probably someone with a grudge and too much drink in them. Perhaps one of your lot."

She rolled her eyes as if this was a later appendix to an old argument. "I doubt it. A nice clean deep slit to the throat isn't really the drunken way. A kicking, a head bashing or random stabbing maybe…"

"You've been reading too many true crime books."

"Not really," she contradicted as she finished off her tea. "Although I will admit I read that new one we got in last week. Really good glossy pictures, you know."

"You're a ghoul."

"I should take that as a compliment." She wandered through into the shop, swinging up onto the revolving stool behind the cash till. Another day of work. Not that she complained much about this job – it was one of the best she had ever had. She got to read most of the day and had persuaded the Professor to set up a second-hand venture for her to run through the shop. Made her feel as though she was actually capable of achieving something.

Dionne switched on the computer screen, watching her reflection disappear as the machine burst into life.

"Did you ever get your instruments set up on the folly?"

With a dull thud the Professor dropped a pile of hardbacked cookbooks onto the end of the desk. "Now that's a leading question if I ever did hear one. You were just thinking to yourself where that man had been killed."

"They still haven't released any details about him, have they?"

"No. And if they're all like Seger, it doesn't take much to realise why," Wagstaff muttered grimly. "I still haven't put my instruments up at the folly, to answer your previous question. Although I'm sure you'll be interested to know that I had been planning on going there on Sunday evening."

She was interested enough to take her eyes away from the computer screen. "You were there?"

"No. I was on the bank, and the folly had been my next stop, but unfortunately I was interrupted."

"Seger?"

He nodded. "Although this time he was kind enough to help me carry the ladder back to my car, so I suppose I shouldn't complain."

Dionne didn't look particularly impressed. "He's a jumped up twat in a uniform."

"Dionne, I'm sure a linguist such as yourself could come up with a more articulate way of expressing that."

"But he's a wa…"

"Not an improvement."

She grimaced in his general direction and turned back to the computer.

"I'll go unlock and let the hoards in, then shall I?" he asked rhetorically, a wry smile on his face. By passing the pyramid of the latest from mass market popular fiction, glancing through the children's books display to note that Sam Seger was loitering outside on the street. It was Wednesday today; that would have been about the right length of time for Sam to realise that he had indeed seen the Professor in the area of the crime scene on the evening in question- three whole days ago.

The policeman looked sharply around upon hearing the key in the lock. Hurrying to the door like a child wanting in the sweetie shop. Wagstaff smiled without any warmth. "I presume this is a business call, rather than pleasure, Mr Seger."

Sam gave him an angry look. "It's P.C. Seger, Wagstaff…"

"Ah, ah, ah," the Professor corrected. "That's Professor Wagstaff." He didn't invite the man in, merely leaving the entrance doors to swing slowly shut. He noticed from the corner of his eye how Sam jumped awkwardly forward to catch one – as if they would lock upon closing – a little put out that the Professor hadn't been more gracious. "I'm to presume that this is about Sunday evening."

"That would be correct." Sam stepped into the first room of the bookshop, looking over the glossy new covers of paperbacks. All these books – wasting time reading. He couldn't understand the need for fiction.

The shop was bright and clean – the ground floor having only been refurnished last year. Dionne was at the back, dark hair piled tousled on her head, sultry looking. Bit of an attitude problem, but a man could do worse, he thought to himself, watching her as she reached across the desk for a book.

"I'm a little surprised you felt the need to come and ask me about Sunday, though," Hammond Wagstaff continued. "After all, you were there with me."

"It wasn't yourself I came to speak to," Sam corrected. "I've been reliably informed that Dionne Nelson was near the folly on Sunday evening."

"What?"

They both turned to look over at the only woman in the building. Dionne angrily slammed the book down. Who the hell had told Sam she had been there? She'd read in the Professor's newspaper yesterday that the police were wanting witnesses and people who had been in the area to come forward. Clutching at straws. She'd had no intention of speaking to anyone about the matter. She didn't know anything, and it was exactly this kind of conversation she had intended to avoid.

"You were in the park, weren't you?" Sam said accusingly as he approached the bench. "Up to your knees in the river. Did you go up to the folly?"

"I did not," she said indignantly. How did he know she had been in the river? He probably knew that she had been panning for quartz.

"What were you doing in the river?"

Perhaps not. She sighed, giving the Professor an exasperated stare as if to inquire whether this was really necessary. "I don't see how it matters."

"You wouldn't, but it might be important."

He was just trying to make himself appear important. Puffing out his chest, looking like a little chicken scratching in the dirt. "I was panning for rose quartz."

Seger looked blank.

She was waiting for him to ask about flowers. "Rocks," she explained.

"How long were you there?"

She shrugged. "Couple of hours." Guessing.

"When did you leave?"

"Got back home at eight-ish."

"Did you see anyone?"

"No," she replied immediately, truculently. "No, wait…" That bloody jogger. So that was how Seger knew she had been at the park. That idiot was obviously of the good citizen variety and gone to the police telling them everything they didn't need to know. "I saw someone out jogging."

P.C. Seger was nodding to himself. "That all sounds about right. I'll be in touch if I need to ask anything more."

Dionne lurched over the counter at the constable started for the exit. "But don't you want to know who I saw? He might have been the killer." A little melodramatic revenge on the stranger for telling Seger she had been there.

"I already know who you saw."

So it definitely had been the jogger who had informed on her. Not that she had been doing anything wrong; it was just the principle of the thing. She held her hands up defensively as she slumped back down onto her stool. "All right. Don't want to tell you how to do your job."

Seger walked smugly out. Wagstaff watched him, shaking his head to himself as the doors swung shut. "I wish someone would."

Quarter to five on a Wednesday afternoon and the shop was distinctly quiet. On the settee in the fiction section sat two men. One was late middle aged, uncut and unruly grey hair being the most striking feature. The other was much younger, a thin man with an acne problem and dusty hands. Cups of tea on the small table in front, they sat each with their book – the man silently reading and the boy speaking, haltingly, his finger heavily traversing the pages as he read aloud.

Jack checked the sign on the door as it swung shut, to check the closing time for a second time. It definitely said five o'clock. He couldn't help but feel as though he was intruding in this quiet, private atmosphere. The lesson in progress, one reading to the other as if the elder was blind.

He had never seen the shy reader before, but he recognised the elder man as the proprietor of the bookshop; a man he had shared short, meaningless conversations of the client-customer sort prior to today. He coughed awkwardly.

The young man was the first to look up, nervous and self conscious, he quickly reddened. The Professor took a little longer to rouse himself from that other world of imagination he had been lost in. He looked blankly at Jack for a moment for remembering himself.

"Can I help?"

"I had a call left on my answering machine," Jack started to explain, wishing increasingly that there was someone else other than the three of them in the building. "One of the books I'd ordered has come in. Is the shop still open? I don't mean to interrupt…"

"Not a problem at all," Wagstaff interrupted, snapping his book shut. "It's our own fault for starting early. There's still fifteen minutes before lockdown." He jumped up spritely and made his way to the customer desk. "What was the name?"

"Jack Dougan."

The Professor set his book down by the till – *The Wind in the Willows* by Kenneth Grahame – and went through the open doorway behind the desk to a small room packed with shelves. Books still to be put on display, orders in alphabetical order by name waiting to be picked up. Whilst the man searched through the

D section, Jack's eyes wandered back to the desk. It was a mountain of disorganised clutter: heaps of new, unsold books, sheets of large paper with bold writing. It looked as though he had just taken down a display. Books on the Highway Code and theory; history of the automobile; road safety; dictionary of accidents. Accidents? Jack turned the hardback book around and peered closely at the title. Sounded like a cheerful read.

Wagstaff materialised at the till. "Our constant travelling companion."

"Sorry?"

"Death."

Jack smiled wryly. "That would be what the optimists would tell you."

"Very true," the Professor commented, setting a hardbacked book with a painting of a wooden war ship on the front onto the desk. He pulled out a piece of handwritten paper from the book. "I have here that you ordered three books, in my very fine scrawl. We've only got this one in as yet. The other two are out of print, and second-hand books are not really my department. Unfortunately my assistant is out this afternoon raiding the homes of the recently deceased." He paused, drumming his fingers on the glossy cover. "Her order book should be somewhere here. I can perhaps find out what stage she's at for you."

"Be good if you could, but don't worry yourself about it too much," Jack said as the professor started to rifle through books and papers under the desk. "There's no desperate rush." He tilted his head, scanning over a ripped piece of paper from the presumed display. It looked like a brain storm; words to do with roads and transport, the motor car, infrastructure, road safety... then a name just caught above the tear.

"Who is Bridget Driscoll?"

"I beg your pardon?" The Professor bumped his head on the desk on his way up.

"Bridget Driscoll."

The man looked blank.

"Sorry, bad habit of mine," Jack gestured at the paper. "I was just looking at the remains of your display."

The Professor looked at the heaps of books – not sold during the promotion and still waiting to be sorted. "Oh, I see," he visibly relaxed. "I just took that down after lunch. If you're interested, I can recommend the Encyclopaedia of Travel Accidents," he said, picking up the volume Jack had just been examining, setting it up on end as if preparing for the big sale.

Jack gave the book a cursory glance for the second time. "You're all right, I think I'll stick to my sea faring adventures."

The Professor nodded in an understanding manner. "Quite agree. That'll be twenty-eight pounds please."

Jack handed over his debit card.

"I haven't actually read it myself either, and I don't intend to," the Professor confessed as he put the card in the chip and pin reader. "But I just thought to myself then, wouldn't it be good if I could sell the last copy. We've actually sold three copies of that book, you know."

"Really?" People would read anything.

The man nodded. "And all in the last month. Those displays do really have an effect."

The machine beeped and requested a pin number. "You still haven't told me who Bridget is, though," Jack joked as he put in the number. "Or do I have to read the book to find out."

"First woman in the UK to be run down and killed by a motor car," the Professor told him authoritively, one eye on the till as he flicked through the hand written sheets in Dionne's search ledger. It looked like a system of chaos, but as long as it continued to bring up results and she didn't expect him to deal with it, he wasn't going to tell her to change her ways.

"Not the way you want to be remembered, is it?"

"Not really. Ah, she has found one of them." He tapped an entry in the ledger. "Doesn't say here when it will be landing though. I'm sure she'll give you a ring when it does."

"That'll be great."

While the Professor took his time selecting a paper bag, shaking it out to insert the book and receipt, Jack turned, leaning against the desk to survey the bookshop. The youth who had been reading had disappeared. Nothing but rows and rows of books. He really ought to have ordered this one off the Internet – it would have been a lot cheaper – but there was an old-fashioned, perhaps romantic part of him that wanted to keep the little oddities (and these days that sadly included the independent bookseller) alive in this world.

His eyes drifted, settling on a small empty table in the next room – the non fiction section – with a bare section of wall above. One solitary drawing pin blotting the otherwise uniform surface.

"How do you think of your themes?"

"My themes?"

"Yeah, do you just wake up one day and think, what we really need to promote is traffic accidents."

"Nothing like a bit of blood and carnage."

"Yeah," Jack laughed.

"I don't think of the themes, the society does," the Professor said, averting his eyes and quietly going through to the annex to put away the ledger, regardless of the fact that it had been under the desk. Dionne would be cursing tomorrow when she couldn't find it. But he wanted to avoid getting into a conversation about this. He wouldn't lie unnecessarily, especially to people whom he considered pleasant and intelligent – and there were precious little of those. The society certainly wasn't a secret, although it wasn't meant to be talked about either. It was surprising how few had ever asked about how those promotional displays came about. And no one had been really bothered about the society.

He turned around to meet curiosity. Jack was leaning over the desk as if he was about to start begging for detailed information. He looked as though this was the most interesting thing he'd heard all month.

"Society? What society?"

The Professor considered the man, trying to think what it was that Jack Dougan did for a living. They'd had a few short conversations over the occasions Jack had been in. Easy going, chatty kind of person. Slightly Australian. He seemed to recall him working at the local flea pit. Oh yes, and he edited some obscure periodical or something to that effect. Oh lord, he recognised that look: the same thing he suffered from.

"The Society of Lost Causes plans the displays," Wagstaff informed him as he returned to the desk.

Jack laughed out loud. "Seriously? Lost Causes? There's actually a society for that? I've never heard of them."

"It's not a national group, just a small, local organisation."

British eccentricity. Jack looked fascinated. "And what exactly does a society for lost causes do?"

"They research obscurities, historical mainly. Saving them from being entirely forgotten." Wagstaff couldn't help himself. There were so few he could really talk to about this, and even fewer who ever wanted to listen.

Jack was shaking his head in amazement. "Bloody brilliant. Do these fellas have meetings or anything?"

"Meetings?"

"You know, meet up and discuss the latest lost cause. Open to the public."

He really shouldn't have said anything. "It's not open to the public, I'm afraid," he confessed. "Very small group."

"How do you join?"

"Well, I..."

"I'm presuming you must be a member, considering you've heard of them. Why else would you have these displays in your shop?"

"I confess, I am," the Professor said, wondering why he felt like a criminal. He'd never done anything illegal, at least not for the society, anyway. "But I'm afraid it's virtually impossible to get into. You have to be recommended by a member. Oh look, it's five," he exclaimed. "I do apologise, but I have somewhere to be – need to be prompt locking up tonight."

Jack smiled conspiratorially at him. "Not to worry, I understand." Picking up his book, he wandered to the exit. "Thanks for the book, Professor. I'll be back when the other one comes in."

As her heart started to thud in her chest, Dionne closed her eyes and tried to command calm. Except that she already was calm, perfectly relaxed. It always did kick off in the quiet moments, her nervousness never appearing in times of stress. Like those planes that could break the sound barrier.

She slunk back into her seat, slouching heavily. Just chill out and watch the film. Her chest tightened. Oh, for crying out loud, she thought, why now? James Stewart's face in close up loomed over her in black and white, blazing out from the darkness. So close. Sat in the front row, almost as if the screen was about to swallow her up.

Come on, girl, she scolded herself. You're here to enjoy the film, escape reality for a couple of hours. Forget your problems. Dionne stared up at the screen and wished she'd saved the money for her dinner instead. But a James Stewart matinee on a Sunday afternoon had been too big a temptation. She'd been out walking by the river, and on her way home on her regular route, she had passed the cinema. The posters had called out to her, and she had found her feet veering around to enter the building. An unresponsive teenager had taken her money and sent her on to the auditorium. And here she was now, watching an old Hollywood legend and wishing that if she could just run up at the screen hard enough, she'd somehow melt though and become a part of the film.

Too late, the credits were rolling up now. The end. Dionne pushed her body into her seat, irritated that people were already getting up, pulling on their coats against the spring afternoon chill. Preparing to leave. She really didn't want to go home. Someone coughed and bumped roughly into the back of her seat as they went for the aisle. She sat up and looked over her shoulder to the auditorium. A lot of elderly people, a few couples and a man in his forties who looked like a stereotypical film buff. These were her contemporaries on a Sunday afternoon.

Out of place, at the back, stood at the top of the aisle with her hands on her hips as if the film had been offensive, was a woman in a trouser suit. Lank, muddy blonde hair. Dionne scrutinised her from the front row. She'd seen her before. Yes, her photograph had been printed in the newspaper on and off whenever the cinema put on a special film or event. The cinema manager. Dionne couldn't recall her name, but she came across as the enthusiastic, career type.

Annoying was another word for it, she thought grumpily, turning back to the screen and folding her arms across her chest. Not that she was jealous as a general rule: Dionne had never been interested in careers, money and status. But considering her life up until now and the way things were going, she would probably have to keep on working until well after she had died. Sometimes she just wished things had worked out a little better. It was weak moments like these when she would regret Filippo.

She stayed in place until the credits had most definitely finished. The sound was switched off; the screen was a blank white with no projection. Nothing more to see. The auditorium lights were on full power. She was outstaying her welcome.

Standing up, she stretched out her body. Picking up her bag, she turned towards the exit. The manager was still present, having moved into the corridor. The door marked private was open and she was talking to someone just beyond, hidden in the start of another maze. The cinema was in an old building, converted for the cause but still riddled with staircases and corridors hundreds of years old. What history this place must have imbedded in its walls.

Dionne approached, her curiosity unable to help itself, she had to peer over the manager's shoulder and through the door.

"I thought I could hear a whirring," the manager was saying.

There was a man coming down the staircase. As he raised his eyes to look at the manager, Dionne realised it was the jogger she had seen a week ago. The good citizen who had told tales to Seger. As if she looked like a murderer. He looked at the manager then up to Dionne as she walked by in the background. A brief moment, then she was gone.

The wind was blowing up a tantrum outside. Dionne wrapped her coat around her and hurried home. They had said the weather would deteriorate during Sunday evening, in preparation for the new week. She'd probably have to walk to work in the rain, she thought pessimistically as she unlocked the door to her flat and stumbled in.

Shaking her coat off, she hung it on the back of her chair. Kicking off her shoes as she went to the kitchen, she boiled the kettle, hanging around to indulge in steam-warmed air. Taking a large mug from the cupboard she took a teabag off the draining board and threw it in the cup. Hues of rust swirled outwards as she poured in the boiling water. She punched at the bag with a teaspoon a couple of times before dumping the tea bag ceremoniously back on the draining board.

Finding her way back through the darkened flat, she entered her bedroom, for the first time flicking on a light. The curtains were still drawn. Setting her mug down on a cluttered bedside table, Dionne hopped into bed, pulling the duvet up around her. It was such a comforting feeling to be snuggled down in bed. She could quite happily never get up again.

The newspaper she had taken from work yesterday still lay on top of the bedclothes. Dionne leant back against the twisted metal bed frame and gazed at the front page headlines. They were still writing about that murder. Of course they would be, it was the most exciting thing to have happened here for years. And the police had just named their victim.

Reaching out, she pulled the paper close and stared down at the photograph of a dead man. In this he was alive, a close up from a holiday snap. Trevor Washington, 38, from Carlisle. He'd been engaged. His fiancée was distraught. She wouldn't dare be anything but, Dionne thought cynically. Her eyes flittered over the details that had been released. They said the risk to the public wasn't too high, in that Trevor had been a specific target. He'd been found with a rather expensive digital camera on him. Obviously not a theft. Probably someone with a grudge had gone after him. Apparently he liked to take photographs, and had gone up to the folly to take pictures of dusk falling on spring time.

Dionne peered questioningly at the photograph, reproduced in grainy newspaper quality. Of all the places, why did you come to take pictures in our little town? Our insignificant little folly that no one outside a ten mile radius had ever heard of. It said in the paper that the couple had planned to come to the town for a day trip together, but the woman had felt ill on the day and he had travelled alone. She wondered if the police were treating the fiancée as a suspect now.

It always was the most obvious person. Real stories were predictable. Glumly, she tossed the paper onto the floor and stretched her feet down the length of the bed. She sipped her tea and listened to the silence. Her day off was always over so quickly, then it was back into another week of routine.

Putting her tea on the table, she lay back in bed. She wondered if she was getting itchy feet again. She had been here for three years. It was the longest period she'd stayed anywhere since leaving home. She'd certainly moved around a lot, done many things. She stared regretfully at the ceiling. Except now she wasn't going anywhere.

From her kitchen window Dionne had a view encompassing the extent of her life. The only omission was that she could not see the bookshop; which to be fair, took up the largest chunk, but everything else was represented. It was a sad state of affairs that this limited span was what it had all crumbled down to.

Her flat overlooked the Geordie's back yard. A cheerful, overgrown elf of a man, he worked at the quarry and did carpentry in his spare time to bring in a little extra cash. The weather was reasonably clement as far as the wood was concerned, and a half constructed item stood in the small yard, against a work bench. Drifts of saw dust collected against the stone wall.

In the distance she could see the pub. The grey rooftops. The greenery of the surrounding hills on the horizon. Her gaze filtered over her little, empty world, and settled on the film crew on the road. The name of a local television studio was printed on the side of the van. This would be on the evening news tonight. Still no fresh information on the dead man's killer. By all accounts, the killing had been particularly brutal. The murder at the folly. Strange that it had been committed there, she mused to herself. Considering the folly was connected to another murder of sorts.

Dionne turned away from the window and pulled her jacket on. She had to get to work.

Mark Grierson, the Geordie carpenter, was leaning against the stone wall with a mug of tea in one paw when Dionne came down the steps from the doorway of her building. He nodded to her, the lank, slightly greasy long strands of hair falling in his eyes. Swilled down the tea. "Morning, there, D."

"Mark." She stopped on the other side of the wall and they watched the television crew. The reporter, in a serious dark grey trench coat, preened in front of the camera, garbling and appearing worldly serious. The man with the boom looked bored. A woman with a clipboard was picking at her nails.

"It hasn't been that exciting, has it?" Mark commented idly, shifting his noticeable weight and setting the mug on the workbench.

"The murder?" Dionne asked absently minded, tilting her head to examine the reporter. She had seen him on the television before.

"Oh aye, the murder. You'd think it'd be all exciting, like. Murder and intrigue." His eyes widened and his fingers wiggled as if he were in the house of horrors. "And the papers are making something and nothing. We've found out nothing more since it happened. They say it was all bloody and that, but the kids haven't been able to find any blood stains up there."

Dionne raised an eyebrow coyly. "I thought that area was still closed off as a crime scene."

"Well, you know what kids are for sneaking in."

"You don't have any kids."

The old man pretended to look distressed. "Dionne, man, you wouldn't turn me over into the hands of the law, would you?"

"I'll think about it."

"I'll buy you a drink at the pub tonight. You are on, aren't you?"

"Yes."

"I shall be putting in an appearance no doubt. You need something for a Monday, don't you?" Mark looked back up their dead end road to the adjoining thoroughfare where the television crew were working. "Aye up," he exclaimed, his Geordie accent momentarily dipping into broad Yorkshire and making Dionne smile. "Watch yourself; I think we've been spotted."

The woman with the clipboard was marching in their direction. At this stage it was presumptuous to think they were the attraction - an overweight fifty-something hairy man and a woman in an oversized second-hand trench coat. The cameraman and sound operator hadn't moved, and the reporter wavered indecisively.

"Excuse me," the woman called out.

It was them she wanted to speak to. Mark straightened his shirt; Dionne shrunk deeper into her coat.

"I'm from North News," she explained, thrusting her clipboard at them as if that would validate everything she said. "We're just filming a piece for tonight's news on the murder. We were wondering about getting a few local views on the matter; see if this has raised any concerns for you. We can't guarantee whatever we shoot will be used, but there's always a chance for your opinions to be aired on television." She was looking at Dionne as she was speaking, who to be fair, out of the two, was the more photogenic. But it was Mark who was getting excited.

"I'll be on the telly?" Mark asked.

The woman looked over at him. "That's the idea."

"I'm up for that."

Dionne glanced at her watch. "I have to get to work."

"Don't you want to see me getting interviewed?"

"I'll see it on the television," she told him, heading up the road. "Besides, it'll give you something to tell me this evening."

The reporter had given up on wavering and acted decisively, following his producer. He smiled at Dionne as they unintentionally approached one another. "You don't fancy being on television?" he asked, wishing it was her rather than the enthusiastic man the crew had heard from back at the van.

"No thank you." She hugged her coat around her body and hurried away from the cluster of people. Get me back to my books, she thought; their voices fading out and the sound of her boots tapping against the pavement taking over.

Mondays were particularly grim, Dionne mused later that day. Slouched by the desk in the bookshop, the soles of her boots propped against the telephone directories on a shelf under the desk, she gazed into the middle distance and tapped the end of the biro on the corner of her tooth.

The start of another week, the long trudge through another six days of work, wondering when she could get back to herself and her own life. Not that her own life had so much meaning these days. Her existence was work, making money. Money: the root of all misery.

It had been a particularly pointless day at work. Barely anyone had come into the shop. A few browsers, virtually no one who actually wanted to buy. She didn't see much point in her having been there at all.

The door opened and a potential customer came in. Dionne made a move to sit up straight, look presentable and eager to help. Welcome to the bookshop, how can I assist your learning today? She then saw it was the jogger who had so kindly informed Seger of her presence at the folly, and slunk closer down towards the desk.

He had not been expecting to see her. He had been sure she was familiar from somewhere in town, but it wasn't until her saw her in this setting that he remembered she was the odd bookshop girl. The bookshop girl – a description which equalled their sparse conversations on the transaction of money for books. Brief and short. She had always seemed a bit distracted, but today he couldn't help but smile at her reaction. She looked as though she wanted to slap him. A scorned lover.

"What are you doing here?"

He knew smiling would only wind her up, but he couldn't help himself. "Is this the way you speak to all your customers?"

She sniffed at his response as if she didn't care, although secretly she was glad that Hammond – Wagstaff to people he liked; Professor to those he didn't – had decided to take the afternoon off. He would have told her she was working too hard and needed to take some time off. Forced her to take holiday.

"You are still open, aren't you?" Jack asked, beginning to wonder if he'd missed something.

"We are," she confirmed coldly. "Although I don't know whether I'm inclined to help police snitches."

Jack laughed loudly. "Snitches?"

"It was you who told Seger I was at the folly when that guy was done in, wasn't it?" she accused. "Where on earth was the point? I didn't see anything. I had to put up with all of Seger's rubbish the other day. That man creeps me out."

"I can see where you're coming from, but it was nothing personal. How long did he bother you?"

She shrugged. "Five or ten minutes."

"At least you weren't persuaded by a well meaning colleague to go and make a statement."

"A statement over nothing?" She raised her eyebrows, appearing to physically relent a little. She supposed Seger would have eventually found out she was there and come knocking. Maybe it was a little premature to throw the jogging stranger into the same box as Seger.

"Something like that. So shall we call a truce?"

"All right," she said begrudgingly, trying not to sound too good natured. "Although it can hardly be a war when I don't even know who you are."

"You did call me."

"I did?" Her kohl-rimmed eyes widened.

"About a book. I'm Jack Dougan. And you are?"

"Your helpful bookshop assistant." She stood up from the stool and wandered through to the back room. His name was familiar. "I do remember calling you. I left a message on your answer phone." Picking up her tome of second hand book orders, she flicked through to the relevant entry. She marked it as completed.

Jack watched the woman with interest as she pulled a hardback volume down from one of the top shelves in the doorway. He barely knew a thing about her, but he was increasingly convinced that his presumption of her eccentricity had been well grounded. Although it wasn't much of an intuitive conclusion to make about someone he'd seen stood in a stream with a sieve.

Dionne set the book on the desk, already bored by the title and look of the front cover. Naval history. Not something she'd been tempted to read on her lunch breaks before the book was collected.

"They still don't know who killed that guy," Jack made light conversation as he passed her the cash for the book. "At least that's as up to date as my local gossip goes."

"No," Dionne's attention looked as though it was drifting again. "I saw a television crew this morning. It's the most interesting thing that's happened around here for a long time."

"Depending on what you class as interesting," Jack commented as she passed him the book. It was a sharp move, signalling the transaction was finished – please go home – but he chose to ignore it. "I was in the other week. Your boss was telling me about Bridget Driscoll."

She glanced back sharply at him. It felt like an age since that display had been pulled down. She hadn't realised this Jack Dougan with his Australian twang and lazy smile had come into the shop enough times to notice Bridget Driscoll and the line up of traffic accidents. He had been paying attention. "Did you buy one of the copies of The Encyclopaedia of Travel Accidents?"

"'Fraid not," he told her. "I just saw the display being taken down." He looked over to the table where the eclectic collection of books had been. Nothing had been laid out as a replacement. "Are you going to be having a new display there?"

"Soon. I'm just getting the poster finished."

"So you make the display. Not the society?"

Dionne's eyes narrowed slightly. He was digging, she had been sure he was digging at something and now she knew what. "How do you know about the society?"

"The Society of Lost Causes?" He made it sound as though everyone knew about it. "The professor told me about it."

"Did he now." She sounded suspicious.

"I'd not heard of them before," Jack continued, watching her reactions with amusement, guessing that she was involved. Not only that, but she didn't want 'outsiders' to know. "Sounds interesting. Historical obscurities."

"It's not just that."

"Is it not?" He pretended to look surprised. "You're a member too, then?"

"I might be." Dionne felt uncomfortable. She felt as though he was making fun of her.

"When's the next meeting."

"It's not a public concern," she said quickly. "Besides, it's only of interest to members."

"The professor told me you could become a member if you were recommended by someone in the group."

Just how much of a conversation had those two been having 'the other week', Dionne worried. Had the professor gone so far as to suggest this Jack Dougan ought to join them? Someone who bought boring dusty books about naval history would be a welcome addition, she thought sarcastically, perhaps a little unkindly. Of course, she didn't know this man, and was no mind reader, but Dionne suspected everything on principle and always presumed everyone apart from her closest confidants was making fun of her. It was a defensive tactic that had taken many years to perfect.

"That may be so," she said, thinking quickly. If the professor had told Jack he could come along, she needed some way to put him off. But what, she wondered as she stared at the reading area for divine inspiration. "But it needs to be seconded by the chair."

"The chair?"

"The founder."

Jack examined her face. Her painted lips. Her nervous fingers. The twist of hair that had come loose from her hairstyle. Her distracted look. She was rapidly growing more and more interesting. And he guessed it was going to take a little bit of work to be accepted into this very small, but very appealing society. "I take it that's you."

She smiled primly. "Yes."

"I see I'll have to work on you."

"Oh, we don't have any space. At least not until someone dies."

"What were you fishing for that night?"

That was enough mickey-taking for one afternoon. Arrogant Australian git. "I have to lock up now," she told him curtly. "And you've got a book to read."

Jack could take a hint, besides, he genuinely didn't want to make an enemy of her. Her – because he still didn't know what she was called. "I'll see you around, my helpful bookshop assistant," he called to her as he went for the door. You couldn't expect to get what you wanted the first time you asked.

Dionne folded her arms, watching him leave, and for a fleeting moment wondered if it was time to be moving on again.

Dionne's Guide to Men – Part One

"*La vaginismus?*" the female Italian doctor had asked, stating it as a feisty proclamation as if slightly merry on alcohol. It was a game of guess-what's-in-my-head. One game she didn't want to play. They'd tried common ailments, depression, anaemia and stress, and now the doctor had moved on to a list of sexual dysfunctions. She didn't feel as though they'd found anything suitable. Her love was like her life and there wasn't a diagnosis. Everything just felt dead.

Dionne clutched her handbag to her chest and felt she was going to be sick. Five minutes later, after a blur of information from the doctor, she was back out on the street, almost mowed down by a speeding moped. The driver casually swerved around her. Dionne staggered backwards and leant against the building wall. Felt her heart hammer against her ribs.

On the other side of the road a tall African had shook out an old bed sheet onto the pavement. There were lines of cheap replica handbags. Something for the tourists and ladies of limited means. Dionne was a lady of limited means – truth be told she was flat broke – but she carried the real deal. She didn't even like handbags as such, but this had been a gift and she felt obliged to take it everywhere with her. Made her look like a real Italian lady, very sophisticated and beautiful. That was what old *Nonna* Lecce had said. With her dark hair and smoky eyes, she could pass for an Italian, just as long as she didn't speak too much.

Later that afternoon, stretched out on the settee with yet another box of chocolates set on her chubby thighs, Dionne glared at the black and white photograph of Filippo and decided this was all his fault. He had flicked a switch somewhere inside her and everything emotional and sensual had shut down. If this was love, she'd rather eat her chocolates. If this was life, she'd rather watch melodramatic Italian soaps.

Of course it wasn't love – not the mutual understanding, the soul mates, the rubbish you read about in sentimental romances before real life gave you a smack on each cheek and introduced you to the way people really were. The longer she stayed in this flat, the less she liked her life and herself, but conversely, the less capable she felt of coping with anything at all. She was trapped.

Filippo adored her. He had no idea who she was, but he had filled in the blanks with his own ideals and aspirations for the future, and that was more than enough for both of them. To him, the fact that their sex life had fizzled out and become non-functioning barely after the start was a mark on his powers, and he was determined to seduce her subconscious reflexes, despite what her body was saying it didn't want to do.

Filippo, the thirty-one year old governmental statistician had, three months before they met, made the first step into life and moved out of the parental home and into a flat of his own. He missed his mother a lot, and would frequently go to visit, at least until he found Dionne. Then he had his princess, his goddess, the woman he would worship and who would bear his children. He had it made.

Dionne had met him three months after moving to Rome. Twenty years old and living abroad for the first time, she had been overwhelmed by life and baffled by full speed Italian, which was like a completely different language to the one in the classroom. She was studying Italian and Icelandic at UCL. It was supposed to be half a year's study at Rome University, half a year at Reykjavik. But life has that way of not following the plan.

She didn't really understand the language full flow, was mystified by the fast and hectic Rome, just as she had been by London. She didn't feel settled in her new life as an exchange student and hadn't slotted into any of the social groups at the university. The Italians didn't mix with the strange breed of foreign students. The exchange students stuck to their nationalities and no Brits Dionne knew had selected to go to Rome. She spent her free time wandering through the centre of Rome, gazing at the architecture, telling herself she was living the adventure. She was cultured and interesting now. Making the most of life. Inside she wanted to run and hide.

She had met Filippo at a café overlooking the Colusseum. It was a busy time of the day and there were no free tables. Filippo had graciously asked if he might share her table. He had noticed her textbook and asked if she was a student. He could hear from her accent immediately that she wasn't Italian, and had been touched by her quaint way of speaking. Dionne had been thrilled that a native wanted to talk to her.

He had taken her out to dinner that very night. She jumped at every offer and suggestion. To actually have a niche of her own. Someone she could run to and escape herself. Filippo had a wonderful city centre flat – heavenly luxury compared to the student accommodation. Quiet, peaceful. He told her she was beautiful. Gave her presents. Fed her chocolates, strawberries, ice cream in the bedroom. She spent more and more time in the flat. Started skipping classes. Two months after their meeting she had left the scruffy student room arranged for her by the university. She quit her lessons and moved in with Filippo permanently. Who said a degree would get you anywhere in life?

It had all been blissful to begin with, playing the Italian's mistress, skipping through the tourists, making drawings of architecture and statues before returning to prepare a meal for her man. Making love in the evening. It didn't last long.

The perfume, the silk lingerie, the slips, the dresses, the jewellery, the handbags... all the fittings of a sophisticated woman. Someone she had always imagined in her head to be another generation and another world away from herself. She grew stifled, not able to remember herself. She didn't go back to the UK for Christmas and her father worried. She learned her language from the day time television. Filippo came home and told her she was beautiful. She felt like a two dimensional painting on the wall.

She lost interest in herself, in Filippo, in life. She felt her skin crawl when he told her how wonderful she was. He didn't know the first thing about her. Her sub consciousness switched her body off to him, and they stayed on separate sides of the bed.

One day whilst watching a holiday programme she was surprised to see a feature on Iceland. She began to wonder about her studies. She had been in Italy little over a year. She ought to be back in London completing her final year. Doing something. Her mind wandered. It seemed a little too early to settle down and stop. But moving on took money, and her reserves had all been spent a long time ago. She lived on Filippo financially just as he lived on her emotionally. Besides, student life was roughing it, and she had grown accustomed to the good life. And Iceland was expensive. Not the kind of thing you could do on a whim.

The night she decided what she was going to do, Filippo came home with a large bouquet of roses for her. They didn't look like a present for her, a twenty-one year old girl who had stopped living. A girl not a woman. Lying in bed, listening to him gently snore, and gazing up at the high, moulded ceiling, she made her plans.

"Dionne, you haven't moved any of the books on order have you?"

Five to seven on a Thursday evening. Late-night opening at the bookshop. Dionne was stood in the staffroom, leaning over a stack of romantic paperbacks to view her image in the mirror on the wall to apply red lipstick. She jumped at the sudden intrusion: sighing in relief when she didn't accidentally paint her cheek in lipstick. She twisted around to look pointedly at the professor.

He returned the stare, a little surprised by her transformation in the five minutes since she had left the shop floor to get ready for her other job. "That's very gothic. Charlotta's not branching out into whoring, I hope."

Dionne narrowed her eyes. "Hammond," she spoke to her employer. "I have not branched out into whoring, as you so antiquely put it, but it may be worth considering. A way to make some extra cash."

Considering her obsession with working, he hoped she was joking.

Dionne put her make up away in her shoulder bag and quickly checked her hair in the mirror. "All the books are where they should be."

"Except for the one I am looking for. Jack Dougan's final book came in this morning. You remember, that black and white one about Viking longships. It's not under D."

Jack Dougan. That sounded familiar. She pursed her lips. "Do you mean that irritating Australian?"

"I find him quite amicable."

"I must have put it under A." She walked over to the shelving, immediately finding the book in question. "For Australian."

"It's very reassuring to know you're not one for turning people into characateurs."

Dionne didn't have time to good naturedly bicker with the Professor this evening. The shop closed at seven and her next shift started at exactly the same time. She was lucky both employers were so understanding.

Jack stopped slouching against the desk as Dionne appeared in the shop like a Victorian Madame. Long black velvet skirt, black silk bodice with floating sleeves, hair tied up with oriental ornaments on pins sticking out like clichéd chopsticks.

"Are you not a bit overdressed for a bookshop?"

Dionne ignored him and looked over at the professor as he emerged from the back room. "Maybe that should have been A for annoying."

"Do you speak to all your customers like this?" Jack laughed.

"Just you. I'm late; I have to get to work."

"You are at work."

She ignored him, hurrying past in a haze of perfume and rustling skirts. "I'll see you tomorrow, Hammond," she called over her shoulder.

Jack looked at the Professor. The Professor looked at Jack. "You'll have to excuse Dionne," he apologised. "She's a bit stressed."

"Dionne?"

"My assistant."

Jack nodded. "She's got a second job."

"She does a few shifts at the *Blacksmith's Anvil*." The Professor placed the book carefully on the desk between them. "You're not harassing my staff?"

"No. I'm a very easy going person. There's just something about your assistant."

"There certainly is. Just don't wind her up too much. She has a lot to deal with. I think she could use kindness more than irritation."

Jack flashed him a smile. "I know when to quit. Now, how much do I owe you?"

Thursday nights at the *Blacksmith's Anvil* were music night. Charlotta had booked folk-rockers Amiss for the night – a curious bunch: Irish fiddle player who looked like a cherub-boy still waiting for his voice to break; a French chain-smoking accordion player who was not happy about the English smoking ban in public places; a Cumbrian guitarist; and a Cornish singer with the longest hair Dionne had ever seen on a man.

The regulars were to be seen intermingled in the crowds, as well as local music lovers, fans of Amiss who had come for this performance and other random passers by who weren't quite sure what they'd walked into. The singer's girlfriend was sat behind a table at side of the room with a selection of CDs on sale. The fans already had the collection and everyone else was waiting to find out if Amiss were any good before parting with cash.

The group were getting ready for the performance. The violinist was tuning his violin. The accordion player sat nonchantly on a bar stool on the stage and played a few notes. Thought longingly about tobacco. Mark Grierson caught Dionne's eye and raised his half-full pint glass to her.

She was tired, and would rather be in bed than running around after a bunch of half-drunk revellers. But the live music nights at the pub were always the best, at least she got to listen to music – not always fantastic but since Dionne's CD player had broken, she had never replaced it and was stuck with whatever the radio stations wanted to offer. The music offered a diversion as well, and kept her going through the final shift of the week at the pub.

Hands stretched widely, fingers clamped to the sides of glasses to keep the collection together and not crashing to the floor, she turned to take the glasses away to be washed. She saw Jack weaving his way through the hoards of people towards the bar. Alone. He appeared as though he was looking for someone. She raised her eyes to the ceiling. She hoped this was just a coincidence and Hammond hadn't blabbed her evening's movements.

Jack turned and saw Dionne staring at him, a little hostile. Perhaps he was getting to the point of pushing this too far. Not that it had ever been that intentional, but people could take all kinds of comments the wrong way. It had never been his intention to torment her, but it was possible that she might think it was.

"Dionne."

She briefly raised her eyebrows, wondering how he knew her name. Hammond, she supposed.

She stepped around a group of twenty somethings and approached the annoying Australian. "I think we need to nip this in the bud. I don't appreciate being mocked."

"I'm not here to mock you."

"But you keep turning up."

"A man has a right to go to a pub."

She didn't look convinced. "Maybe. I have work to do now."

A loud note from the violin came through on the loud speakers. The violinist leaned forward to the microphone. He wasn't one for presentation, introductions and amusing chat. "This is one from Sweden," he told the slightly inebriated crowd. "It's about a train."

Distractedly, Dionne's attention left Jack and gazed back to the stage. What a random thing to come out with. The music immediately started, fast and rolling – violinist, a guitar player who had appeared at some point, the accordion player with the same lethargic stance and expression, his arms seemingly moving independent of his body. She looked back at Jack to say something, but he had gone. She wondered if she had jumped to conclusions about him.

For a folk music session, it was surprisingly upbeat. There were only two sad songs that Dionne counted, and a lot of instrumental sessions with fast gigs and reels. For all the developments in both composition and instrumentation there was still something to be said for going back to acoustic and traditional music. The evening was busy, and Dionne didn't get many opportunities to just stand and watch the musicians. She listened, submerged in the sound.

At half ten the session ended and people started to drift away. The bar thinned out. Mark Grierson and a couple of colleagues from the quarry were at the bar talking to Jack – did they already know each other? – laughing about something. Mark shouted across the bar at Dionne as she finished serving a customer.

"Got another story teller here, D."

She walked down the bar to the drunken gathering.

"Your friend here has been telling us tales of sailors in the South Seas."

One of the men she could never remember the name of sniggered into his beer like a seven year old who had just heard the word sex spoken out loud for the first time. Dionne raised her eyebrows: 'her friend' – just what had he been saying?

"Oh right," she said, looking from Mark to Jack. "I can't say I know any stories about sailors in the South Seas."

"You don't?" Mark turned to Jack. "Our Dionne knows stories about all sorts. She was telling us about this woman killed by a car going at four miles an hour the other week."

Suddenly she was tired of hearing about Bridget Driscoll. She didn't want to get onto any subjects connected to the society whilst Jack was here. "So what about these South Seas stories?" she asked, looking directly at Jack.

"Maybe a bit too risqué for repeating," he smiled at her.

"Ahoy! One of the lads!" Mark shouted, pounding his pint glass on the bar. "I'll tell you one about this German lass I went out with once. The things she could do with a grape…"

"Will have to wait for another evening," Dionne interrupted, taking the pint glass. "We're closing up soon. You know we never have time for stories on music night."

"Oh aye," Mark turned to Jack. "You'll have to get yourself here on a Tuesday evening."

"Did I ever tell you about that time I saw the cat?"

All but one in the small crowd of men surrounding Mark Grierson stared blankly at the Geordie quarry worker and spare time carpenter. The one who clearly knew what Mark was talking about – the one Dionne could never remember the name of – tried to breathe in his next gulp of beer and almost choked in the effort.

Alan, the youngest in the group, glanced uncertainly at Dionne. She didn't often see him in the pub. She generally only saw him at the bookshop when he came for reading sessions with Hammond, or when they were having a society meeting. Alan didn't talk much about deeper motives and emotions, but she guessed that he didn't feel completely comfortable with the quarry men, despite the fact that they had been his work mates since he had left school at sixteen. They were burly men hanging around the middle aged point, rough with life, full of experience and practical knowledge. Alan was still a gangly young, self conscious and constantly looking terrified that someone might find him out. He didn't really fit in anywhere.

As well as the two older quarrymen and Alan, Jack had joined the group this Tuesday evening. The four of them were lined up along the bar, settled in for the night.

"Have I not told you this one, D?"

Dionne, on the other side of the bar, paused in stacking up clean glasses. "Do you mean Mrs Appleton's cat?"

"Mrs Appleton?" Mark paused, confused, before it dawned on him which cat she meant. "Oh, man, no, not that cat." He looked around the group, pausing for blatant dramatic effort. "This is a different cat."

"Well, get on with it, Mark. We're all waiting."

"It was last summer, in June," he began his story. "I was walking home. You all know where I live? Near D's place. We're near the fields. Well, I had this feeling I was being watched. Man, it was like ice being poured down my back."

"Are you not embellishing this slightly?" Dionne asked.

"This is the god's honest truth." Mark protested. "You're too cynical at times, D. Do you find it impossible to have a serious conversation with her?" he asked Jack.

"It can be."

"Well, back to my serious story."

"Serious!" the nameless quarry man sniggered.

"Give it a rest, man," Mark complained. He loved the attention. "Back to this cat. I stopped and looked over at the wall. There was this cat looking over the wall at me."

The quarryman was laughing into his pint. Dionne, Jack and Alan looked as though they had missed the joke.

"You don't like cats, then, Mark?" Jack asked. "I can't say I could be doing with one around the house."

"I don't mean a house cat. Not some soggy moggy sat on a wall. This was a big cat." He demonstrated with his hands like the fisherman and the one that got away. "A big black cat. A panther."

"Oh Jesus, Mark." Dionne sounded unimpressed. "You're trying to tell us you think there's a big cat roaming about round here? Like the beast of Bodmin?"

"The black cat of the Yorkshire Dales." Jack raised his glass to that.

"You haven't asked him where he was walking home from." The quarryman said.

"Where were you walking home from?"

Mark shrugged innocently. "The *Blacksmith's Anvil.*"

"So you'd been drinking."

"You sound like my mother. Besides, you remember last June? I was off the beer."

She flicked mentally through the last months. "Was this when you were trying to be more cultured?"

"Oh aye."

"And you thought drinking red wine would be the thing to do."

"It was when he was chasing that bird from the council," Mark's workmate eagerly added.

The rest of the group were laughing now.

"So you were drunk?"

"I'd only had a glass."

Dionne just stared at him.

"Or two." Mark shrugged. "I might have been a little bit intoxicated, but I know what I saw."

"Mark, that story was rubbish."

"All right, D, the night is young. You do better."

"And what story would you like to hear?"

Jack put his glass down on the bar. "How about the one about Jonathan Martin?"

Dionne paused in what she was doing and looked directly at Jack, surprised to hear him mention that name. Jonathan Martin predated Jack even asking about the society. How would he know about it? The display wasn't up yet. But she had been drawing one of the posters yesterday and Jack had been in the shop, although she couldn't remember why. He must have seen the name there.

"Right, let's hear about Jonathan Martin," Mark agreed, knowing nothing about this story. "Who is he?"

Dionne pursed her lips, feeling she'd been hijacked. "Was," she told Mark distractedly. "He's dead now. He was a nutter in his time."

"That's a theme for this evening."

Mark shook his head. "We have nothing in common."

"You're from that same part of the world. He came from round Hexham way. That's near Newcastle."

The laughing started up again. Mark finished his pint. "It's all relative. Now tell us about this Jonathan fella."

"Yeah, did he see big cats on walls?"

Dionne smiled weakly. "No, but he did see God."

"Even worse."

"Shut up, will you," Mark snapped at his work mate. "I want to hear the story of Jonathan. And can I have another one?" He pushed his empty glass towards Dionne.

"So Jonathan Martin," she started, noting how a silence fell down upon them, like children waiting for the bedtime story. She started to pull a pint for Mark. "Was born in the late 1700s up round Hexham way. When he'd grown up, he set off to London, but things didn't go to plan and he was press ganged into the navy. It was during one of the battles that he took a nasty knock to the head."

"So that's when he became a nutter."

"Thank you, Mark.

"When he got out of the navy, he headed back up north, got married, had a son and worked at a tannery. He started having visions of God, of his dead mother coming back to him and letting him know he was going to come to a bad end. He got in with a religious group, the Ranters, and started a campaign against the mainstream clergy, who he thought were corrupted. He'd hide in churches and pop up during services and start ranting. He got so carried away that neither his family nor the Ranters wanted anything more to do with him. His wife eventually told the police about him, and he was carted off to an asylum."

"That's women for you," the quarryman commented.

Dionne gave him a cold glance as she passed Mark his pint. She had always been a little wary of the nameless quarry man. There was a streak of cool harshness in him that she had never liked.

"So was that the end of Jonathan Martin?"

Jack's voice made her jump. She looked across at him, having forgotten he was there. "No," she answered. "Friends helped him escape. He was caught again, then escaped and no one seemed bothered about locking him up again. He wrote his life story and toured the area selling his booklet.

"He was getting madder and madder, and his visions were getting worse. He moved to York and had a dream about a big black cloud settling on the Minster. So he decided he had to burn the place to the ground.

"He went into the Minster during a service and hid. He waited until everyone had left the building, then he ripped up some of the cloth décor there and some books and started a fire. He smashed a window and jumped out."

There was a particular hush over the group.

"York Minster's still there, though," Mark pointed out. "Did the fire just go out?"

"No, it was really bad. No one realised what had happened until the next day when the fire was really blazing. The woodwork from the 1300s was lost, the organ destroyed, a music collection gone forever, etc, etc.

"It didn't take long to work out that Jonathan Martin was responsible. He'd sent threatening letters prior to the arson attack. They caught him a few days later and he was put on trial for the destruction of York Minster. He agreed with everything the prosecution said. Everyone agreed he was guilty, but the jury declared him mentally insane. He wasn't hanged, but sent off to a mental asylum for the criminally insane and spent the rest of his days there until he died."

Silence.

"The end."

Mark sipped at his pint. "Nutters, eh?"

Dionne lowered her eyes. She sometimes felt people just didn't understand the fascination with historical anecdotes. Of a curiosity and a thirst for the details behind an event; the obscurities surrounding a story; the sheer randomness that made life so rich. Somewhere Jack watched her.

"They're saying a nutter killed that bloke up at the folly," the quarryman spoke up; glad the barmaid's odd story was finished. He wished she wouldn't hang around with the fellas as much as she did. "They say there's no motive or anything for it. Just a frenzied stabbing."

"It happens sometimes," Mark nodded gravely.

"Smithy was joking it was old Eddie, at lunchtime," the quarryman continued. "You know what Eddie's like. A bit weird. You could imagine him doing something like that." He pulled a stupid face and pretended to stab at thin air like a mad man.

Dionne looked away in distaste. Making comments like that in situations like these was just irresponsible. In less enlightened times it was this kind of half-arsed drawing of conclusions that got innocent people lynched. She felt grateful relief when she saw someone new approach the bar. "I have to go serve this customer," she told them, hurrying down to the other end of the bar.

"Eddie's all right," Alan muttered quietly.

"How would you know Eddie didn't do it? Is it because you stabbed that bloke?"

The others were a little taken aback by the sudden viciousness that had cropped up into the conversation. Jack felt uncomfortable. He didn't really know these people all that well, but had taken them for easy going types. Alan looked terrified. Mark just looked bored as if he had heard this all before.

"Give it a rest," Mark told his work mate. "You know Alan's matey with Eddie. It's getting late now and we've got to get to work tomorrow morning."

"Sounds good to me." Jack finished his drink and got up from the bar stool. He tried to catch Dionne's attention, but she was now deep in conversation with the landlady. She distractedly waved goodbye to the group, then turned back to her employer, her face serious, her arms folded.

Hunched over the desk, Dionne was copying the ordnance survey map of the town onto tracing paper. In the background Hammond chattered on the phone in the staff room. Technical, weather-related terms interspersed in the conversation, laughter at someone getting confused between two similar sounding words that – according to two wise old men – ought to be obviously different. The meteorologists discuss. The British were reputedly obsessed with talking about the weather, but this was just being ridiculous.

Dionne glanced over her shoulder. Hammond was oblivious to the world. Lost in thoughts of fluffy clouds and air currents.

When she turned back to the shop, Jack was walking into the building.

Dionne checked the clock. Half past nine. She looked back at Jack. "Do you not have a job to go to?"

"Not till five," he told her cheerily.

"Five?"

"I work at the cinema. I'm the projectionist."

Of course, she had seen him there before, talking to that woman who managed the flea pit. Dionne put her pencil down. "Is that the only job you have?"

"Are you worried about my finances?"

"Not that it's any of my business," she started, sounding as casually disinterested as she could. Truth be told, Dionne was curious about everyone's finances. How many hours they worked, how much money they made, how much their living costs were, how they managed to do all they did and if they ended up in the red at the end of the month. If there were any clever tricks she didn't know about. She never dared ask people directly about these things but she could never switch off from this minor obsession of wanting to know.

"Thing is," she continued. "The cinema only shows a few films a week and I can't imagine there's a lot for a projectionist to do when he's not projecting."

"True enough, it is just a part time job. But it's more than you might think. For every film you watch, I have a good three hours of prep. But I have my other job. I run a periodical."

"What do you mean you *run* a periodical?"

"As in I run it. I am the editor, the proofreader, the treasurer, the finance manager, the layout editor and part time article writer."

Dionne tried her best not to look impressed. He was proving to be more than she had first presumed. "And what is your periodical about?"

"It's called *Naval and Seafaring History.*"

"Ah. That would explain the books."

"It would indeed. If you like, I can give you a few copies of the magazine."

"No!" Dionne burst, perhaps a little too quickly. "Not my thing. No need." She didn't want him to think she was looking for freebies. "So why are you here? We haven't got any books in that you ordered. Is there something you wanted to order?"

"No."

"Something I can help you with?"

"Not book related. I just came by to say hello. And to thank you for the story last night. I didn't really get to speak to you much."

"I was working."

"Yeah, you always seem to be working," Jack sighed. "Is there ever a time when you're not working? When do you get time off?"

"Not very often."

"Are you at the pub again this evening?"

"No, I don't do Wednesdays."

Wednesdays when they had a screening every week. "Come over to the cinema then. You ever been back stage so to speak? The projection room. It's quite interesting…"

"No." She looked distracted.

"Seriously, it is. I thought you were interested in random things."

She wasn't paying attention at all. He turned around and saw the man in the entrance. A man who was completely out of place. He looked like a London civil servant from the fifties, in a very well tailored suit, complete with the handkerchief peering out of the jacket pocket. He had a grey broom moustache, neatly trimmed hair, a black umbrella hanging in the crook of his elbow. A bowler hat in the other hand. A bowler hat for Christ's sake. Was this going to be some kind of surreal talking telegram or a general joke? Certainly not, because the man looked awkward, not even sure if he had the right to walk into the shop.

"Dionne, are you all right?"

Dionne looked as though she'd just been slapped. "Dad."

Dad? Jack looked back around at Dionne. He had to admit he had never really thought about what kind of people had produced someone like Dionne, but left to his own imagination, he would not have thought of this.

As if pushed by invisible hands, Dionne's father walked up to them, bumbling and awkward.

"Dad," Dionne repeated, still not over her surprise that her father was in the shop. "What are you doing here?"

"I was worried about you," he said, carefully setting his hat on the desk. "I haven't heard from you for weeks. I've tried calling but I keep getting this ridiculous automated message that your number is no longer in service."

"Oh, yes, that," she muttered, realising she ought to have thought of a back up plan when she had cancelled the phone. "I'm between phones. I will get a new land line soon."

He didn't look completely convinced. "Why haven't you got a phone now?"

"I wasn't happy with the service," she lied. "But you didn't need to come up to check on me. You didn't need to drive all the way from York."

"Of course I did; you're my daughter."

Dionne was feeling increasingly uncomfortable. She didn't want to have to have this conversation with her father, and she definitely didn't want to have it whilst Jack was here. He had not taken the hint and left. Anyone with any decency would have walked out. Family issues were private matters.

"I haven't seen you for a long time."

Oh Christ, parental blackmail. "I will come and see you soon. I need to go down to York to do some research."

He brightened at this. "When?"

She was being pushed into a corner. "I'm not sure, as soon as I can get a lift."

"You could get a bus down to Northallerton and take the train. Come and stay a few days. This professor must let you have some holiday sometime."

This was too much. "No."

"I'll come and pick you up."

"No, I'll get there on my own steam."

"If you can't afford it, I'll gladly pay the travel costs."

Please, Daddy! She screamed inwardly. "I can afford it," she lied. "I will come soon. I promise."

"Make it soon."

An awkward silence settled down. Jack still hadn't left. It felt as though he were watching them like a street-performed soap opera. Her father was trying to appear jolly but she could see he was still a little upset by all of this. She was going to have to go and visit soon. She couldn't think her way out of this right now. Visiting would probably mean taking time off. And how would she get there? She was falling off the tight rope.

Her father didn't like awkwardness. He was looking at Jack out of the corner of his eye, noting that he was still here, drawing the wrong conclusions. "I don't believe we've met."

Jack smiled at him. "Jack Dougan."

"Graham Nelson." They shook hands. This cheered her father up immensely. Dionne could see the cogs in his head whirring. Jack was mulling over her family name – the naval connections undoubtedly setting the cogs in his own brain in motion.

Her father looked at her. Dionne was becoming defensive. "Jack's an acquaintance."

"We're mates," Jack said, for a moment slipping into broad Australian as if he'd just rolled off the plane. He looked as though he was treating this all as a big joke. "So you're from York?"

"Oh yes," Graham said. "I work for Allertson and Co."

Jack looked blank.

"They're a tailoring company. Very well regarded. Go back generations. I'm a tailor."

"Really."

"Yes."

More awkward silence.

"You should come," Graham told Jack. "Every gentleman deserves at least one tailor-made suit in his life."

Dionne wanted to cry. She wanted to tell her father that this was no gentleman. She said nothing. Watched it all in mute horror.

"A suit?" Jack considered the idea. He had a couple of off-the-rack suits for interviews, funerals, weddings and other such formal occasions that rarely ever cropped up. Most of the time he was to be found in jeans and casual shirts. He wasn't really in the line of work where you needed to dress to impress. "Not a bad idea. I'll have to drop in on you sometime."

Dionne had an awful feeling he wasn't just being polite. She had to get her father away from Jack before any more damage was done. "Look, Dad," she started. "Why don't we go get a coffee somewhere. I'm sure Hammond will let me go for my lunch break early." She twisted slightly, seeing the Professor still on the phone.

"Hammond!" she shouted at him. "I'm going for lunch. Now. Early."

The Professor looked surprised for a moment, caught sight of Jack in the background, then smiled and nodded and waved her off.

Thank god. Dionne picked up her bag from under the desk and slipped around to the other side. She picked up her father's hat, as was her habit, and set it on her head. "Shall we go, then?" she asked, slipping an arm through his. "Jack won't take offence if we leave now. He was heading off for work anyway, weren't you, Jack?"

He realised that he probably should have departed a while ago. "Yeah," he nodded, pretending to look at his watch and realising he'd left it at home. "I must be really late now. Got to dash."

It all went straight over her father's head. He smiled politely at Jack. "Very nice to meet you, Mr Dougan. I do hope we meet again soon."

Dionne compared the street map she had traced earlier in the day with a copy of a town map from the early 1800s. The old map wasn't exactly to scale, so it wasn't the easiest of tasks to always compare the two down the precise positioning of buildings. She had walked down from the market cross in the high street that was marked on the old map. According to what appeared correct to her, she ought to be standing outside the old police house and prison.

She looked up and stared across the road to the cinema and the deli next door. Somewhere in there was the cell where Saskia Weaver had spent her last night alive.

The architecture on this block of the high street looked reasonably old. Dionne wasn't an expert, but the faded painting on the wall above the deli looked like Victorian advertising. It was certainly possible that some formation of the cellar level cells still existed, but on the other hand she supposed the buildings that had been converted into the cinema would have been gutted to accommodate this relatively modern house of entertainment.

"Dionne!" Jack called from the other side of the road. He waited for a car to pass before crossing over to her. "Are you thinking about coming to see the film tonight?"

Dionne glanced up from her maps. Would that man not leave her alone for five minutes?

"You can come and watch it from the projection room if you like."

"No thanks."

"Doing a bit of surveying?"

"No," she sighed. She should have checked the time of the films before coming down here. She watched as a woman she recognised as the cinema manager walked up the footpath towards the cinema. She gave Dionne and Jack a curious look before stepping into the building.

"I'm just trying to work out where the old police house was. You don't know anything about the cinema building, do you?"

"Oh yeah, that was a prison or something once," Jack told her. "There's a couple of old cells down the bottom. Amanda usually keeps it all locked up. Health and safety."

"Really? Do you think I'd be able to go down there and take a look?"

"Depends," Jack answered, knowing full well it wasn't up to him, but he didn't need to point that out to her right now. "Whose life story are you investigating now?"

"Sorry?"

"Well, we had Jonathan Martin, and that woman who was hit by a car before that. It's for that society of yours?"

Dionne felt uncomfortable. She didn't like talking about the people and events they looked into until all the information was collected. Even then there were few she could comfortably open up to. "Does it matter?" she asked. "We'll change the display and put new posters up eventually."

"Come off it, Dionne," Jack laughed. "What's all the secrecy about? I think it's interesting, what you do. Would it really hurt that much to tell me?"

She supposed it wouldn't hurt to let a few details slip. "We're doing Saskia Weaver," she relented. She didn't even know why she said 'we'. The society consisted of herself, the Professor and Alan. Alan was only there because Hammond seemed to have taken him on as a project. Hammond was there because he was one of the few people she really properly knew here and he supported the eccentricities of the world. But she was the only one who really bothered to do anything. Finding the facts for the stories she could then tell.

"So Saskia Weaver was a criminal?"

"No," she shook her head, gazing across at the cinema. The cinema manager was still loitering in the foyer, watching them. "She was the last person in this town to be executed for witchcraft."

"Really? I've never heard of her before. So what did they do her – drown her in the river?"

Dionne smiled tightly. "Our river? Hardly deep enough for that. She was burned at the stake. She spent her last night alive in one of the cells there."

"I'll see if I can get you in there to take a look then," Jack said, pleased that she had told him. "Tell you what. We've got a screening Saturday afternoon. Why don't you come over an hour before?"

"I can't. I'm working."

"Working? Are you ever not working?"

"Rarely feels like it." She nodded at the cinema. "I think your boss is waiting for you."

"What?" Jack looked distractedly at the building, catching sight of Amanda before she shrank further back into the depths of the foyer. As if they'd just caught her out. He turned back to Dionne but she was already walking away.

"See you around, Jack."

Inside the foyer, Amanda was behaving as though she had one long itch up and down her body. She walked back up to the glass panelled doors and peered back out.

"You all right, Amanda?"

"Yes," she muttered, distracted as she watched Dionne's retreating figure. "That was that strange woman from the bookshop, wasn't it?"

"What, Dionne?"

Dionne. Amanda inwardly rolled her eyes. Even her name screamed 'look at me!' She hadn't known that Jack was friendly with Dionne from the bookshop. "So what were you two talking about?"

"Witches."

"Witches?" Amanda smiled wryly to herself. "That would be about right. She strikes me as a bit of a witch."

"Have you two got a feud going?"

"Oh no," her eye's widened. She didn't want Jack to think she was the bitchy type. "She just comes across as a bit odd. I don't know her."

"She's doing some research into the local history of this place," he told Amanda. "About the police house that used to be here. Wouldn't mind a look down at the cells if that's all right?"

Amanda looked a little horrified. "You're the second person to ask about that today. Some weird little guy with a mouth full of spit was asking this morning. God knows why. Said he was from Northallerton. I told him no."

Jack laughed. Amanda's take on the world could be a little impatiently strange at times. "But I'm not a little man with a mouth full of spit."

She glanced over at him as she moved away from the doors. No, you're not a little man, she thought. "Health and safety. It's a fire risk."

"Fire risk?"

"Well, you know what I mean. There's only one way down there. If that staircase got blocked by a fire there'd be no way out. People could burn to death down there."

"I'm sure we'd survive the experience."

"I can't let members of the public down there," Amanda re enforced her point. "Don't you need to be getting the projector ready?"

He could take a hint. "Better get on with it," he said to his boss, bowing down to her superiority on this occasion and heading off up to the projector room. Perhaps the creepy little man with the mouthful of spit – whatever that was supposed to mean – had unsettled her enough to make the old cells in the cellar an unwelcome topic of conversation. He'd leave it a few days then give it another go.

Stretched back in the chair, her feet propped up on the small table, Dionne chattered into the telephone. She was in the back room, swallowed up in a large collared woollen jumper dress, strappy sandal dangling from one of her feet. Oblivious, discussing god only knew what with a Russian customer based in London. She'd started learning Russian a couple of years ago, and since she'd reached the stage of daring to try out her skills on unsuspecting natives, her Russian-language client base for the second hand Internet based venture had really expanded. The Professor didn't suppose for a minute that she spoke the language as if it were her mother tongue, but she could chatter at a fair speed and the customers were probably charmed by her attempts. That and intrigued by the Russian-speaking eccentric selling books from the Yorkshire Dales.

She hadn't noticed that a customer had been waiting at the cash till to buy a book. The Professor was sat with Alan at the front of the shop. They had taken a pause whilst he had gone to finish the sale. Another hardback copy on the history of York – the display on Jonathan Martin, historical York, lunatics and religious fanatics was doing a reasonable trade.

He returned to the settee and picked up his copy of *The Wind in the Willows*. They were a good two thirds through the book now. It was the current choice for their small reading group. A group of two, not for the literary appreciation as such, but more for a focus on the actual art of reading. When the Professor had first met Alan, a gawky eighteen year old staring in through the bookshop window, he could barely read a word. It was such an awful notion that someone couldn't pick up a book and enjoy it, that he decided he was going to make sure the boy could read. It was terrible that there was still illiteracy in the UK despite all the compulsory schooling, but it still happened. Alan could read now. It was stilted, but it was improving.

Dionne appeared behind the front desk. She had managed to sell an obscure Russian book she had been lucky enough to pick up on a trawl through a house clearance. A tidy profit.

Sitting down at the desk, she turned the local newspaper around so she could flick through it. The murder of Trevor Washington was still managing to make it into the news, but it was struggling. The bloody murder was three weeks old and the police had literally no new leads. The fresh excitement of carnage had most definitely gone stale. No one had any idea who had committed the murder, or why. With a few weeks, it almost felt as though it had never happened. A large percentage of people still avoided going up to the folly, but local teenagers had crept up to see if the dead man's blood still stained the earth.

Dionne had heard that the victim's two brothers were coming to the town to drum up support and get the mystery solved. Unhappy with the feeble progress the police were making and the fact that the television crews had grown bored with nothing new to report, they were making news themselves. They would stamp their feet and thump their chests; storm through the town until someone confessed or the clichéd clue they were convinced was out there, turned up. No doubt there would be a press conference when they temporarily moved up here.

Idle local gossip said that it was a lunatic who had committed the murder. Must be a man, a bit of a loner. Awkward, found it hard to fit in or talk to people. A real freak. Eyes roved outwards, inspecting their neighbours and colleagues, wondering if it might be someone they knew. It was best to find the murderer as soon as possible. No knowing if a nutcase like that might have acquired a taste for blood.

Pushing the newspaper away, already irritated, Dionne looked up and watched Hammond and Alan, hunched over their respective copies of *The Wind in the Willows*. The Professor's charity case: Alan the illiterate boy. She was impressed by the progress Hammond had made with the lad, although in all honesty she didn't know whether she would have had the patience or interest to help someone to that extent.

They finished the chapter, ending the lesson for that day. The Professor set his book to one side. "Sold another one of the books from the display whilst you were on the phone," he told Dionne.

"Really?" She raised her eyebrows. They had sold five books off the display and it hadn't even been up a week. Perhaps it was the picture of a cathedral burning that caught people's eyes. Show them drama and carnage, and they were sucked in, wanting the details.

"Have you got much on our friend Saskia yet?"

She smiled wryly. "A bit. I want to go to the archives in York."

"You could visit your father whilst you're down there."

"That was the plan."

"Do you want some time off?" The Professor tried to make the question sound casual. The fact was, Dionne never took time off. She was territorial about her work to the point of being frightening. She worked in the bookshop six days a week. When the Professor had suggested getting a local kid in to help on Saturdays, Dionne had almost attacked him. She would work Saturdays. He didn't need to hire anyone else. Monday to Saturday with full days and late night opening on Thursdays. Then she did three shifts at one of the pubs on top of it. He knew that she took on dressmaking commissions when she could as well – making prom dresses and custom made wedding dresses for the local women who had a bit extra cash for something special. She was coping at the moment, but he had seen her loose weight over the last year and no one could keep that kind of pace up indefinitely. He didn't know why she pushed herself so relentlessly, and when he had asked, he had been met with silence and a look that told him never to bring up the subject again.

"I'm not sure when I'll go," Dionne answered. "I need to find a way to get to York."

Of course there were many ways to get to York. Take a bus, take a train, rent a car. He suspected she meant a way that wouldn't cost her any money.

"Do you know," he started, ever so casually. "We may have to have another meet up soon. We don't have anything planned for after Saskia, do we?"

Dionne yawned, inwardly cursing that it was only Monday. She wanted to sleep. But she had a shift at the pub after here. She wouldn't see her bed until midnight if she was lucky. "No," she answered. "I haven't had time to think of anything. You?"

The Professor shook his head. "Although if we wanted a little fresh perspective on the matter, I know someone who might be able to help."

Alan looked aghast. "I haven't got any ideas."

The Professor smiled. "You're already in the society. I was thinking more of someone new."

Dionne raised her eyes to the ceiling. "Has he been pestering you again?"

"Actually no," the Professor admitted. "I think he's focusing all his time on the source, so to speak."

"Who's this?" Alan asked.

"Dionne's irritating Australian."

"He's not so bad."

"Oh?" The Professor pretended to be surprised. "Are you relenting, Dionne?"

She eyed him suspiciously. "I may have jumped to conclusions too quickly. I'm not saying anything though. Certainly not about the society."

"But you'll think about it?"

She pursed her lips. "That's all I'll promise."

Dionne had taken her lunch break in the local library that Wednesday. She sat at one of the three reading tables in the small library; a stack of books and open notebooks in front of her. A pen lay to one side, and she had been taking notes, but not any more. Her head propped up by a bent arm; she was engrossed in what she was reading. A mix of officiously neat and loosely casual: her hair neatly pinned up in a ball on the back of her head: the secretary-look; the loose jumper dress and sandals precariously strapped to her feet looking as though they were ready to fall off her body.

He wouldn't have come in if he'd known she was here. Not that he was avoiding her, rather that he didn't want her to think he was stalking her. Never mind. Jack leant against the information desk and watched Dionne, who in turn was unaware she was being observed. The librarian – the only one on shift at the moment – was helping an elderly woman select some suitable romances that weren't too crude. At least that was what she was loudly saying to the librarian, but perhaps she just wanted the 'wrong' kind of books pointing out to her for later reference.

Jack had come in to drop off the latest edition of *Naval and Seafaring History*, just back from the printers. He liked to think it was his charitable nature that donated a copy of every edition to the library, but perhaps it was just fear that if he didn't, every copy would eventually end up in the recycling bag. Before heading off on his maritime adventure, Jack's old colleague had told him he was foolish for giving away a free copy – there were at least two old men in the area who read it for free in the library: two potential customers. So slight was their readership that every statistic counted.

Dionne audibly sighed and stretched her legs out horizontally under the table. She stood up and walked up to the ladies, her healed sandals tapping like a dancer's shoes on the hard floor.

The librarian still hadn't noticed his arrival. Not able to help himself, Jack sauntered up to the table like a thief, and looked down at what Dionne was doing here.

A book on local history – a heavy and dusty looking tome that probably didn't make for exciting reading was closed on the table. There was an A4 notepad open, with Dionne's notes in ink. He noted the name Saskia – not surprised by the appearance. She had told him about Saskia Weaver the other day. Not very much, but a brief introduction.

Directly in front of the chair a magazine she was half way through reading lay open and waiting. It looked vaguely familiar. Glancing up to check he was not being watched, he reached out and lifted the left hand side of the magazine to see the front cover. *Naval and Seafaring History*. Two editions back in the illustrious publication of the journal, he thought to himself, already purposefully forgetting that he hadn't immediately recognised what it was. He couldn't help a smug little smile. He flicked through the first few pages, noticing that on the contents page someone had underlined his name where it stood announcing him as the editor.

Guiltily, he set the magazine back in its original position and returned to the information desk. He didn't want to get caught snooping.

Dionne came out of the ladies, pausing at the back of the room when she saw Jack Dougan slouched at the information desk. The same heat frazzled pose he would take up in the bookshop. Maybe he had a thing about women and books. Maybe he visited the librarian just as frequently, she suddenly thought, glancing over at Mrs Harpen, a fifty-something woman with a Victorian school teacher look. She shook her head; shake some sense in there. What did it matter if that even was the case? She didn't care.

He hadn't realised she was here yet. She had time to tidy up. She tapped her way back to the table.

"Hello, Jack."

He turned around. Dionne was stood at the side, smiling pleasantly at him. She was holding the heavy book and the notepad, but the magazine had vanished.

He pretended to note the title on the book as if he didn't already know what it was. "Dionne. Doing a bit of researching?"

"What?" She sounded surprised, before looking down at the book she held. "Oh yes, just a bit on my lunch break. What are you doing here?"

He held up the latest edition. "I donate a copy of every edition to the library. I think there's a couple of old guys who like to read it."

"That's very charitable of you."

"The library has a back catalogue of the last couple of years if you're interested."

She shook her head. "Sorry, not really my thing."

He smiled. The private joke. "Right."

Dionne didn't see what there was to be amused about. "I've got to get back to work."

He let her take a few steps towards the exit before remembering something he wanted to ask her. "Oh, Dionne."

She stopped, turning on her heel. She didn't say anything, just looked questioningly at him.

"I was thinking of driving down to York tomorrow. Didn't you say the other day you were looking for a lift down there?"

Tomorrow was Thursday. Her face dropped. Even if she did accept the kindness of Jack Dougan, presuming there was no ulterior motive, Thursday was not a good day to go. "I'd have to miss two shifts," she finally said.

"Sorry?"

"And it's late night opening at the shop. You wouldn't go at the weekend?"

He hadn't realised his own plans were up for negotiation. Still, she did look as though this was the only way she was going to get to York. "I can't. We've got three screenings on at the cinema."

"Oh right." She looked down at her feet. Sunday would have been ideal. She didn't work then.

"I could go see your dad on Friday," he offered.

Friday could have some potential. She'd only have to take holiday for one normal shift at the bookshop. If Hammond would let her at short notice. He probably would. He was always complaining that she never took holiday. "That could work." She paused. "What do you mean see my dad?"

"Your old man suggested I go down and visit him at his work sometime."

She looked horrified. "*You* didn't have to take him seriously."

"I've already told him I'm coming down."

Dionne closed her eyes, collecting herself. This was getting to be a little too intrusive. On the other hand, he was just visiting a shop to make a purchase and everyone had the right to do that. She could hardly chase away business from her father's work.

"All right," she said steadily. "Friday. But we have to set off early."

Jack grinned. "No worries."

The man bent over the guitar had fingers that danced over the strings with a speed beyond human comprehension. It didn't seem quite right that someone could play a musical instrument that well.

Distracted, Dionne took another sweep over the faces in the pub that Thursday night. She had presumed Jack would come again this week, but he had not appeared. He had attended the last two music nights. At this point in the evening, they were almost half way through the set: no one was going to arrive at this hour.

"D, you lost something?"

She stared at Mark for a moment as if he was speaking a foreign language. "No, sorry, I'm fine. Just a bit tired."

"Soon be the weekend," Mark grinned.

She wished it was. She still had Saturday to get through. Her eyes started to roam again. Mark and that man from the quarry she always forgot the name of were sat at the bar. They had split somewhat over the last hour, due to an interest in two newcomers. Mark hadn't been overly concerned with what they had to say and listened to tonight's performance instead; but the man seemed desperate to gossip. And not in a nice way.

The newcomers were the brothers the grapevine had warned were coming to town. They had driven up from Carlisle that morning and booked into a local bed and breakfast. Already the journalists were returning to the story, and the men had spent the day striding through town shouting into local television cameras, pinning up crudely prepared posters, asking for information and accosting locals, demanding they tell everything.

A death in the family would affect anyone – even estranged siblings would feel a hollow sensation at the very least – and one had to sympathise. Their brother had been brutally murdered for no obvious reason, and whilst the police failed to discover who was responsible, they would always feel as though their grief would never end. But there was something unsettling about these two, as if they were begging for a punch up.

She didn't like to judge a book by its cover, to use a worn out cliché that fitted her profession well, but they looked like mindless thugs. Stocky, well rounded men; eyes pushed into doughy flesh; short cropped hair. One of them had a couple of studs in one ear. They didn't look like they had a kind thought for anyone. They were grieving and distressed, but Dionne found it hard to imagine them any other way.

One of them was looking at her as though she were a hunk of meat he wanted to devour raw. Dionne wished she hadn't put on the long sleeved corseted top. It wasn't revealing, but it did cling to her curves in a particularly provocative way. She was well aware of this, not that she had worn it for any particular reason, but the effort was getting all the wrong results.

"You seen our Trevor about here, darling?" the man asked her.

Dionne was temped to ask who Trevor was, just to play dumb, but she knew better than that. Trevor Washington: the murder victim. She shook her head. "Never saw him." The way he looked at her didn't make her want to confide that she had actually been in the park on the night of the murder. Despite the beautiful music, it was becoming an increasingly horrible environment to be working in.

The man didn't seem particularly bothered that she couldn't help. He continued to stare at her body without apology.

The guitarist offered his thanks for a wonderful audience and set down his guitar. He would be back in half an hour to finish the set. No more music. Just talking. Conversations started up again. Charlotta reappeared behind the bar as people started to return for more drinks.

The quarryman was talking to the brothers again. "It's stands to reason. Some bloody nutter did it. Some maladjusted freak show."

Dionne glanced sharply across at him. That was a big word for a small minded man.

Mark tapped his glass against the bar. "Can I get another one in, D?"

"Sure." She stepped across to Mark, trying to block out the conversation going on beside him. Snippets came through: "freaks"; "bloody headcases that should have been shot at birth"; "there's always one"; "I know a few round here I wouldn't put it past". She gave Mark a concerned look as she pulled another pint. "Doesn't this kind of talk worry you?"

Mark looked back at her. "They're just letting off steam."

"They're throwing accusations around." She didn't like the way the brothers carried themselves. As if their sibling's murder made them celebrities. As if everyone ought to know who they were and show some respect.

"D. Their brother was murdered. I think you've got to give them a bit of slack."

Maybe, she thought as she set the pint on the bar. Her ears picked up Alan's name being mentioned, and she glanced sharply at the quarryman, hoping he wasn't trying to give them some irrelevant leads. One of the brothers grinned at her. "Come on sweetheart, get the drinks in."

Dionne felt ill. She really wished she didn't have to work at the pub anymore. She turned away from the bar and caught Charlotta's attention just as she'd finished serving a customer. "I need to go out back for a couple of minutes. I don't feel brilliant," she told her boss, heading for the back corridor.

Charlotta nodded, looking from Dionne to the brothers waiting to be served. "All right, darling," she agreed, irritated that Dionne wanted a break now, just when they were getting busy again. "But you shouldn't dress like that if you don't want that kind of attention."

Dionne didn't have an answer. She hurried down the corridor, keen to get away from it all.

Last night had taken it out of her; unsettling in many ways. She hadn't slept well; worrying over the things she had no control of. By the time her alarm went off because she was going to York today, she felt ready to die.

It hadn't taken long to fall asleep again. Slouched down in the passenger seat, legs curled, her head slumped against the door of Jack's old car; she made for dull conversation on the drive down through the Dales to flatter land and onwards to York. She had plaited her dark hair in two long pigtails which lay lifelessly on the baggy jumper she was wearing. That and the scruffy jeans made it look as though she was really planning on roughing it.

He glanced over at her as he dropped down onto the A1 motorway. She had looked tired and distinctly stressed when he had picked her up early this morning. From outside the bookshop. Dionne hadn't wanted him to go to her home – he couldn't think why because he supposed if he really wanted to, he could find out where she lived. But Dionne had been adamant that they would meet at the bookshop, so that was how it was.

As the car pulled to a halt, Dionne's head slipped onto the door window sill with a thump and she woke up. Dazed, she peered out of the window, squinting. This was most definitely not York. There was grass on one side of a dusty road, a verge and a fence neatly marking the back of a line of gardens on the other side.

Jack was taking the keys out of the ignition.

"Where are we?"

"You're awake," Jack said, stating the obvious. "I was beginning to think you were ignoring me. We're in Boroughbridge. Just a five minute job; don't mind do you?"

She stretched her legs as far as she could before her feet hit the foot well. "Why Boroughbridge?"

"I've always seen these devil's arrows marked on the map but I never knew what they were. Just fancied taking a look."

"The devil's arrows," she muttered to herself. If she'd been more awake she would have known immediately. "They're big rocks, aren't there?"

"Certainly big." He nodded at her window.

Dionne twisted against the seatbelt and stared out of the window. The road ran down the side of a narrow field where crops were growing. Two very tall megaliths emerged from the ground like Stone Age sky scrapers.

"Big rocks," she mumbled as she tumbled out of the car.

The light bit into her eyes as she walked over to the field, following the trampled track around the edge and up to the rocks; tall and long like clumpy arrows shot down from the heavens. Either that or plunging out from the earth aimed at the skies above. Reaching the first one, she put her hand on the rough, grooved surface of the rock and ran her eyes up the long shaft. She supposed there would be a lot of this rock in the ground as well, foundations to prevent it from tumbling over.

"Must have had a bloody compelling reason to heft these things up into position," Jack commented, standing a little way off from the megalith, hands in pockets as if he dare not approach.

Dionne turned and looked back the way they had come. "The third one is over there," she said, pointing to a clump of trees away from the field. "They're all in a line. I remember coming here when I was little."

"You don't know why they were built here?"

She shook her head.

"Not something your society has looked into?"

Dionne smiled coyly. "Maybe I'll suggest it next time."

It took them another forty minutes to get to her father's house. Dionne's father lived quite close to the city centre, just a little north of Monk Bar. He had a two storey town terrace house with a long thin garden out the back. There was a separate garage on the road opposite the front door. Dionne told Jack he might as well park across the garage door – her father wasn't going to be driving anywhere today.

Leaving Jack with instructions on how to find her father's place of work – trying not to dwell upon what the two of them would talk about; she had walked into town and gone to the central library. She had booked the relevant archives in advance – papers from the landowner who had built the folly. Information she hadn't been able to get hold of at the library in Northallerton.

By lunchtime she had read most of the papers and run out of concentration. She packed her notes and wandered out onto the street. The sun was blazing. It was really hot; surprising as it wasn't the height of summer yet. She pulled off her knitted jumper, feeling the air filter through the thin fabric of her baggy gypsy top, and walked the short distance to the entrance to the Museum Gardens.

There were a lot of people in the park. Office workers making the most of the good weather, filling up every available park bench. Dionne wandered a short distance along the path, before verging off onto the grass and selecting an unclaimed spot. Dropping her jumper to the ground, she lowered her weary body and opened her bag. She had a bottle of water and some unappetising home made sandwiches to keep her going until dinner. She took the food out and set it on her lap, staring at it but making no move to eat. A pigeon nodded its way towards her in the hope of crumbs until she shooed it away.

She eventually forced the food down and crossed her legs to re read one of her old paperbacks. She looked down the bank at the crowds, spotting Jack wandering along eating an ice cream. Sunglasses on, hair casually brushed back, jeans and t-shirt: he looked in his element in the summer. He turned in her direction, and she supposed he had seen her, although it was impossible to tell with people with sunglasses on. She put up her hand to say hello.

He started to walk towards her. "You get all measured up?" she asked as he sat down next to her.

"Yep," he confirmed. "Although I seem to be a bit bigger than I though I was." Certainly not the size he had been back in the dumpling days, but he hadn't been out running as much the last few weeks and maybe it was showing ever so slightly. Either that or he had never been as slim as he liked to think.

"So you thought you'd eat ice cream?"

"Yeah," Jack laughed. "You finished at the library?"

"Yes," she said, watching as he took another bite of the ice cream. He was about half way through. She couldn't remember the last time she had eaten ice cream. There had been a time when she had seemed to do nothing but. Back in the days when she had lived in Rome. Every day had been a *gelato* day then. "Is that good?"

"Oh yes. They're selling them over there." He waved his arm absently in the general direction. "Go get one."

"Oh no, I couldn't."

He looked at her over the top of his sunglasses. "This is a case of if you buy it, you'll get fat, but if it's someone else's, it's all right?"

Dionne's eyes widened. "Oh no, I didn't mean that," she said, still staring at his ice cream. She hoped he didn't thinking she had been hinting for him to buy her one. She certainly hadn't meant that.

He looked from her to the ice cream and back again. "So you want this one?"

"Well, if you don't want it."

He cracked a smile. He hadn't really been offering. "It's covered in my germs."

"I'm sure I'll survive."

Dionne finished off his ice cream. Jack stretched his legs out down the grassy bank. Watched a grey squirrel run up a tree. He told Dionne a little of what he'd talked about with her father. Mentioned that he'd been invited to dinner at the family home. He'd half expected Dionne to shrink back into her hostility but she'd merely shrugged and supposed it was only fair considering he'd given her a lift all the way to York.

They stayed in the Museum Gardens for the rest of the afternoon, before ambling back to Dionne's father's home at five. Graham Nelson was already there when they arrived, unpacking a bag of groceries in the shady kitchen. Dionne said she'd help him cook, and they both refused to allow Jack to remain in the kitchen, ushering him through into the living room to sit in solitude.

He could hear the sounds of conversation, but not the words. In a way, even in this room, he was intruding. The impression he had was that they didn't meet that often, and with references to a now cancelled phone line, communication wasn't exactly easy. They didn't need a newcomer in the way all the time.

Jack remained in the living room – a high ceiling affair with green, thoughtful walls, and pondered on the photographs. There was one of Graham a good deal younger but still formal and very well attired, looking as though he'd just won the lottery. Pride didn't begin to describe the expression. Beside him was a pretty young dark haired woman holding a baby – presumably Dionne. The woman certainly had a look about her that Dionne would get when she stopped worrying. Beside the photograph was another of the trio; this time Dionne was a toddler.

Then the woman disappeared from the photographs and it was just Graham and the little girl. A sombre mood seemed to have dropped onto the pair. Dionne gradually grew taller, becoming more recognisable as the woman he knew today. A woman with large red hair suddenly appeared in the pictorial line of life: a couple of solo pictures before she attached herself to Graham. Then a line of the three of them; Graham Nelson in a tuxedo, the woman in a ball gown and Dionne glowing in a long strapless shimmering dress, all three of them grinning like idiots. A formal graduation picture of Dionne from a university he didn't know about. A picture of Graham, Dionne and a man with a facial jewellery stood in front of a large waterfall. Another picture of Graham and the red haired woman. Then nothing more.

Beyond the conversation in the kitchen, the house was silent. Jack guessed the red haired woman wasn't part of this photo story anymore either.

"Dinner is served."

Graham had appeared in the doorway without a sound. Jack turned from the photographs.

"I see you're looking at the collection." Graham joined him at the mantelpiece. "That's Maggie," he said, nodding at the red haired woman. "This is her house. All I have left of her now. I was very lucky to find her. I didn't think I would after Dionne's mother. She died when Dionne was only four." He coughed abruptly, awkwardly. He really shouldn't be talking about such things with someone he hardly knew. "Shall we go through?"

Dionne was already sitting when they went into the dining room. The food was laid out, steam curling off the surface. She looked mildly distracted. When she saw her father's expression, her look turned to worry. "Is everything all right?"

"Of course it is," her father said as he sat down at the table. "Shall we eat?"

Vegetables and wine were passed around the table. Graham looked unsettled, trying to forget recent memories. He looked over at Dionne. "How long are you staying?"

She seemed surprised at the question, lost for an answer. "I don't know." She looked at Jack. "Can I get a lift back with you? What time were you going?"

"I hadn't thought. Anytime suits."

"You can't go back already," Graham protested. "You've only just got here. I've barely seen you."

"I have to work tomorrow," Dionne sighed.

"Saturdays as well? Really, I think this man is working you too much."

Dionne stared down at her plate.

"Well, at least sleep the night," Graham looked over at Jack for some support. "You can't drive all that way now tonight. Set off tomorrow morning. We have plenty of spare rooms. You're very welcome."

Dionne looked as thought she was ready to walk out right now, but the old man was desperate. Jack nodded, running a finger around the top of the wine glass. "Well, I have drunk a bit."

Graham brightened. "Excellent. You'll stay the night."

"What time do you open tomorrow?"

"Ten o'clock," Dionne said quietly.

"All right. If we head off at eight, we'll be back in time," Jack told her. "No worries."

Dionne could have slapped him.

The mood did improve during the course of the meal. They gradually brightened, became more talkative. Time went quickly. Jack could have stayed with them longer, but excused himself early on, claiming to be tired. In truth he felt as though he was intruding; wanting to leave Dionne and her father alone for more time to catch up. He went up to his room for the night and laid on his back on the bed, staring at the ceiling in the dark. Thinking about everything that had happened.

It was a long time before he drifted into sleep.

Dionne's guide to men – part two

Dionne slipped back into the kitchen sink and winced as the taps dug into her back. At least she had bothered to clean the sink last night, she thought, and wasn't currently sitting in a layer of slime.

Brushing her tangled hair back off her face, she buttoned up the over sized shirt and twisted to gaze out of the kitchen window into the back garden.

Outside, Thorolf was releasing pent up aggression by screaming at an unknown and unseen force. Shoulders thrust back in a particularly macho pose; he was knee-deep in the snow, completely naked and steaming hot. His scruffy red hair was spiked like demon horns. The muscles in his back were taught. Oblivious to the minus degrees celsius temperature.

Dionne was glad she'd decided to stay indoors after their early morning session in the kitchen.

Thorolf Arnkelsson – for that was the lunatic's name – looked like a dangerous renegade eccentric with his wild red hair, pointed devil beard and silver facial jewellery. He even had his nipples pierced with Nordic knotwork silver rings.

Dionne had met him in a Reykjavik nightclub half way through her year's studies at the University of Reykjavik. He had homed in on her, and she had been unable to resist his unusual brand of charisma. On this study abroad she was managing to hold her own with the language, but everyone immediately heard she was a foreigner and wanted to practice their English on her. Thorolf thought it was hysterical that she was even bothering to learn Icelandic, and told her that night under the pulsating lights and smoke that she was going to be his woman. She never really had a choice in the matter.

He had gone home with her that night in the wee small hours, howling at the moon. Since then, they had been in one another's beds almost every night. He was probably clinically addicted to sex, but she didn't feel inclined to broach the subject and quite enjoyed his frenzies. When he was randy – which was often – he could not get enough of her. Once the sexual energy was spent, he was ambivalent to her; never said he loved her and never, ever bought her flowers. She was not his adorable, perfect goddess, and Dionne loved him for it.

When she met him she was a student at the university, and he was a tour guide. He worked for a small travel company that ran adventure trips into the wilderness of Iceland – snow scooters, off road driving to glaciers, geysers and massive boulders reputedly thrown there by the giants of old. Trips across the barren and chilling interior. He drove like a maniac and said he didn't care about a thing.

The fact under the madness was that Thorolf was an economics student. As was the way in a lot of Scandinavia, he would complete one year's worth of studies, then go off and work for a year or so in a random job before returning to complete another year of studies. There wasn't the same kind of strict programme that Dionne was used to with the UK, and it meant that Thorolf could spend a good decade over getting his degree and jumping from work as a guide, a rubbish collector and a nightclub bouncer, as and when the mood suited him. One day, he might just settle down and fall into the role of a financial advisor. Dionne couldn't see it happening anytime soon.

In the end, Dionne lived with him a little over six months, physically exhausted and mentally drained by the end of it. Her bank account was also noticeably smaller, as Thorolf didn't believe in gentlemen always picking up the bill.

She left him in September, packing her belongings the day after he had headed out with friends for a long weekend camping trip in the wilderness with the mosquitoes and beer. When he wasn't fucking her, he was like a passer by on a busy street, barely interested or doing anything for her. He said he didn't care whether she stayed or left – since the university had closed for the brief summer and Dionne's academic Icelandic year abroad had been completed, she had been debating whether to take more time out from her degree and live with Thorolf or go back to London and get the damn degree finished for good.

Of course, the time with Thorolf wasn't constantly terrible. When he was randy and trying to get her clothes off he could be incredibly attentive and talkative. He made her feel like the most important and desirable woman on the face of the earth. It was a frequent and enjoyable experience, but the flame always went out abruptly.

After Filippo, she had always said she wanted someone like Thorolf, but now she was stuck with this aggressive little man who never bought her presents and wasn't making plans for the wonderful family they would create, she didn't feel as though she was going anywhere.

She came to the eventual conclusion that men in general were a bad idea – romantically speaking at least – and it really wasn't worth the effort. Celibacy and concentration on developing her own self and life seemed better. She moved back to the UK and started on her final year at university.

Six months after she had departed from Iceland she got an email from Thorolf asking what had happened to her.

The Professor had come into the bookshop that Saturday. He didn't usually work Saturdays, but claimed that he needed to finish off a large order for the next month's stock. Dionne didn't believe him for a minute. There was a look on his face that was crying out for gossip.

He came through from the staff room with two mugs of tea at eleven o'clock. The order book was untouched at the back desk.

"So how did the research in York go?"

"Pretty good," she said, taking the tea and wrapping her hands around the mug. It was a reasonably sunny day, but she felt on the verge of shivers. "They had quite a few papers from the old Holburn estate."

"Ah, yes, Holburn." The Professor nodded. "They were the family that owned a lot of land around here."

"Did back then. They lost it all a couple of generations after Andrew Holburn." Dionne gulped down her tea. "Thing is, I've read a lot of local superstition and hearsay, countless references to Andrew Holburn, but never anything he'd written until yesterday."

"Did it put a new spin on things?"

She shrugged. "Not so much in that the result was the same. Saskia Weaver was tried for witchcraft and burned at the stake. It was the usual line up of accusations: crops failing, miscarriages, curses and poxes, blah, blah. A lot of wild accusations but no one ever had any evidence for anything. Mass hysteria had taken over and all the locals with a problem took her as a scapegoat. She was a bit eccentric, woman in her twenties living alone and still unmarried..." she faltered, noting that the description was resembling her now.

The Professor politely pretended not to notice.

"She'd turned down a few men who ended up in relative positions of power. I've read in a few places that she was particularly beautiful. They called her a siren. Seducing men to do wicked things. They were baying for blood. There wasn't really ever going to be any other outcome.

"Andrew Holburn, the lord of the manor of the time, was obsessed with science and reason and didn't believe a word of it. He stood up for her, tried to reason with the locals. Everyone wanted her dead for one reason or another. She was sentenced to death, dragged through the streets and burned to death. They said her screams went on for hours; longer than most people set alight remained conscious."

"She was a red head, wasn't she?" the Professor mused. "They say red heads feel more."

Dionne thought of Thorolf. He had never really suffered from emotions. Not in the usual sense. Maybe he had been so acutely in tune and she had been too dull to notice.

"And then Andrew Holburn built the folly on the hill."

"Yes," Dionne nodded. "To her memory. There's local legend that he took the ashes and put them in the foundations. He had the tower built without any door or entrance, so that no one could disturb her again. Rest in peace. They say the ashes melted into the earth and the rose quartz you can find in the river is actually Saskia Weaver. The bones, the memories or the tears depending on which version of folklore you choose to believe."

"And when the wind howls around the town, it's actually the tortured screams of Saskia Weaver; her body in a trillion pieces, blown all over the place."

Dionne opened her mouth to say something, then stopped as a woman entered the shop. It wasn't exactly a national secret, in fact, the stories were there to read for anyone who could be bothered to look, but the history of Saskia Weaver had all but vanished from local memory these days. She waited until the woman had wandered through to the next room before continuing.

"Holburn's children and grandchildren squandered the fortune and the estates and land were broken up and sold off. The park and the folly are common property under the council's care these days."

"So what did you find out from Holburn's papers? Some scandal? Was he having an affair with Saskia Weaver?"

Dionne smiled weakly. "No. But he was always adamant that she was innocent of any wrong doing. Some of the books said he had fallen in love with her, but that was never substantiated, and I never read a word of it in any of his letters. Besides, the man was over fifty when it happened."

Hammond shook his head, amused by her outlook. "Time goes quicker the older you get. And believe me, when you get to fifty, you won't consider yourself past it all."

"Thing is, whilst he defended her and said she had never done anything wrong; he never said she wasn't a witch. I just thought maybe it was because he didn't want to use terms like that, being a man of science."

The Professor was a little confused. "So he thought she might be a witch?"

Dionne shook her head. "He was convinced she was."

"But that makes no sense. He defended her."

"I know, but what he always said was that she was innocent of any wrong doing. He didn't believe any of the accusations the locals had put forward. But I found one letter, dated a few years after her execution where he admitted that although she had done no one any harm, she was a witch. 'She was not one of us'; those are some of the words he used. He said she could evoke the dead. He claimed he had witnessed with his own eyes and could think of no other explanation apart from the fact that she had supernatural powers."

They were silent for a moment. The Professor put his tea down. "You don't believe that do you?"

"Of course not," Dionne scoffed.

"I was worried for a moment you were going to offer a new theory on the murder."

"The murder?" She was so lost in history she had temporarily forgotten about the recent murder up at the folly. "Of course not. That will just have been some random headcase."

"Good. I worried you were going to suggest the ghost of Saskia Weaver slipped out of the folly and killed the man."

Dionne laughed uncomfortably. "Don't be ridiculous." The worrying point was not so much that a ghost was responsible, but that a living person was. Someone who was still free to roam wherever they pleased.

"And you had a good trip down to York? Jack didn't annoy you too much?"

"The trip was fine and he actually managed to be quite pleasant. He was very nice to my dad as well." She caught Hammond's eye. "He went to see my dad at work. He'd suggested he should go and get a suit."

"He suggests that to every man he meets."

"And they all think that because he's awfully British and formal that he's not doing the salesman line." Dionne grinned. "Well, he isn't in a pressurising way; he does mean it in a good way. And he is right; a good tailored suit does wonders for any man. Whether it has to come from Allertson & Co is an entirely different matter."

"And every woman loves a man in a suit."

"Well, yes."

"You do seem to have been spending increasing amounts of time with our friend Mr Dougan of late."

"Hmm." Dionne glanced at him from the corner of her eye. "And there's nothing to draw any conclusions from."

But when Mark brought up the same subject later that day, she started to wonder if she really had been closing her eyes to something more.

Dionne was perched on the brick wall on the side of Mark's yard, yet another cup of tea in her hands, kindly supplied by her neighbour. Mark was taking a break from working on a made to measure wardrobe for 'some rich-bird' who had retired up to the Dales and bought herself a funny-shaped house. Dionne had just been telling him about Saskia Weaver and the new things she had discovered reading the Holburn papers at York city archives yesterday.

"Bloody funny going on," Mark agreed, supping at his tea. "Makes you wonder what could have happened to convince a man like that she was a witch."

Dionne snapped her fingers, pleased he was getting the point. "Exactly."

"Mind you, women are a funny lot," he continued. "There's no accounting for them sometimes. Anyways, what are you doing telling me all of this now? What are we going to talk about on story night at the pub now?"

She shrugged. "Something else. Besides, I don't know how long that is going to last. It wasn't such a great atmosphere on Thursday night."

"Did you not like that fella on the guitar?"

"Oh, he was very good. I meant those two brothers. All the gossiping and finger pointing."

"Don't worry yourself about it," Mark advised. "Those two are just getting over their brother's death. You've got to cut them a bit of slack." He paused, watching her as she swilled the last of her tea round and round in her cup. "You were just a bit put out because your mate didn't turn up."

She looked up sharply. "What?"

"That funny Australian fella, what's his name?"

"Jack."

"That's the one. You two seem very matey. Have you hooked up? Should I be calling him your fella now?"

"Certainly not."

Mark roared with laughter at the expression on her face. "Me thinks the lady does protest too much."

She could feel herself bristling with irritation but told herself to calm down – it would only encourage Mark even more. She put the cup down on the workbench and slipped nimbly off the wall. "Besides, I gave up on men a long time ago. It's much better being independent."

Wrong thing to say: Mark was laughing even more. "Give over, D. You make it sound like you're well past it. I bet you've not even hit thirty yet."

"I'm twenty-nine."

Mark slapped his thigh. "Exactly. Get on with you. You know what you need a bit of."

"Sleep," Dionne muttered, marching out of his yard. "I'm going home now, Mark. Thanks for the tea."

"Not a problem," Mark called after her. He turned back to his woodwork, shaking his head. "Only twenty-nine," he chuckled. "Bloody hell."

Half an hour before the Sunday matinee, whilst Amanda was having a to-do with one of the ushers, Jack happened to be passing her office and noticed the keys to the kingdom hanging in plain view. The keys to every door and lock in the building, including the prison down below. Amanda wasn't going to be in on Wednesday – she was going on a trip somewhere and as she'd only be able to make it half way through the evening's performance, she didn't think it worth bothering with at all. Information that could be very useful in the right hands.

Jack stood and looked at the box of keys. The keys looked at Jack. He decided she wouldn't miss the one to the cellar. Besides, there were two, so he was only borrowing the spare. He pocketed the key and wandered on his way to the projection room.

Sunday's matinee that week was the old Hollywood classic *High Society*. There was quite a turn out – not just people who remembered the film from the original release, but film buffs and younger locals wanting something upbeat and cheerful. Although the weeks had lessened the worry over the murderer, it was still there in the back ground like a threatening stranger.

The film finished promptly at five; another hour and the celluloid was back in its canisters and the projection room looking a lot more ordered than he usually left it. He was ready to go home. Amanda was loitering in the corridor, having sent the ushers home. She appeared uncomfortable as if she had forgotten to say something. She relaxed a little when Jack came down from the projection room. Christ, he thought, she's going to have a go at me about the cellar key.

"Jack," she greeted him as if she had just remembered his name. "Everything go all right today?"

"Yeah, great," he nodded, keen to go home.

"Have you heard the latest news?"

"News?"

"About the murder."

"I wasn't aware there was anything more."

"You know, about the latest theory being that it was a roaming mad man who did it."

"I didn't think that was new."

Her smile dropped slightly. She was blatantly and embarrassingly fumbling. She had been trying to think of a good way of getting this all going throughout the entire film and this had been the best she had come up with. She was falling on her face already. Jack must think she was an idiot.

"It's worrying to think he's still out there. Roaming, looking for his next victim." She gazed out of the doors and tried to look more genuinely distressed than she actually was.

Something was clearly bothering her. He wasn't stupid enough to think it was actually who had murdered Trevor Washington. Jack usually had time for anyone, but today he wasn't in the mood. He opened one of the front doors. "I wouldn't think about it too much, Amanda. There'll have been a motive. You won't be next on the list."

She stumbled forward, her ring of keys rattling. He couldn't get away now that she had found the courage to start this. "It's still a worry though, isn't it? I live alone and I've got to admit I've been more jumpy at home the last few weeks. It's not nice walking home on my own either. I keep looking at vans and wondering if someone's going to drag me into one." What was she saying? This was getting worse. She was hurriedly locking up, well aware Jack was walking down the cinema steps to the road; conversation finished, each going their separate way.

"Jack," she started desperately. "Would you walk me home?"

He looked back at her if she'd lost the plot. "I think you'll be all right at this time of the day."

"I want to talk to you."

His shoulders dropped, a twinge of guilt. She did look wound up. He could spare her ten minutes. "All right," he relented. "I suppose I can play hero for a bit."

Amanda grinned widely. "Thank you."

Amanda lived in a neat little cottage up a steep hill on the edge of the town. There was a small grassy area where children sometimes played football, then a short line of cottages above it. A footpath started at the end of this little dead end road, moving through a copse of trees and across windswept grassy fields overlooking the town. You could walk up the Dales through to the next villages from here.

"You know, I think we should go out to dinner one evening next week," Amanda blurted out, barely daring to look at Jack to see what his reaction would be.

He nodded thoughtfully at the suggestion. "Like a cinema crew outing."

"I suppose." She didn't really want to think about it with work connotations.

"When were you thinking?"

"I don't know," she said breathlessly, surprised this was going as easily as it was. He was so laid back about it, as if he had already taken all this as a given a long time ago. "Just sometime during the week. We can just take it when and how we feel. Don't even need to decide where yet."

"I think we do," Jack contradicted as they started up the steep road to the line of cottages, the last of which was Amanda's. "Just to make sure there'll be enough space. There'll be, what, eight of us?"

"Eight?" Amanda sounded horrified. He thought she meant a work's outing.

"You were going to include the cleaners, weren't you?"

Damn, damn, damn. "Yes, of course."

Up ahead, at the end of the road sat a woman on a public bench. Rather than admiring the view, she was leaning forward with her head between her knees. The pose rather depicted how Amanda was feeling right now. The woman looked up at the sound of their approach, not wanting intrusion on the private moment of suffering. Amanda recognised her as the woman from the bookshop. She panicked and did the only thing she could think of. She put her arm through Jack's.

Dionne looked up and saw Jack with Amanda, the woman's arm through his, and felt something pull her upper ribs inwards towards her spine. She didn't want to see this, especially at this moment in time. She was finally feeling better, as if she'd now manage the short walk back home. She was tumbling back down the hill into the black terror.

She had slept in late that morning, crawling out of bed at lunchtime, and decided to go for a walk in the hills. She had been feeling particularly buoyant, upbeat, and looking forward to whatever was to come. Her body was relaxed, her mind unconcerned. And as she had walked along the high path back into town, a minor panic attack had hit. She had sat down on the bench to calm down. She hadn't suffered from one for a few weeks. She had believed that she was getting back on top of things. Perhaps she had relaxed too much.

"Dionne?" Jack called over to her. "Are you all right?"

No, she wanted to reply. I think I'm going to throw up. Feeling like an idiot, she stood up, waved awkwardly at them, then turned and headed in the opposite direction – unfortunately back out into the countryside. She couldn't face walking past them. Risk of polite conversation. Never mind, she could swing around and drop back home the other way.

Jack watched her figure march away into the field, her open jacket flapping in the wind. A lonely stick figure retreating into the distance. Amanda pulled on his arm. "I think she wants to be alone right now."

He wasn't convinced, but didn't argue. Just watched with concern.

Amanda shook her head to herself. "She's a weird one," she muttered.

The hairs on the back of his neck prickled. He glanced around at Amanda, then down at her arm clinging on to him, wondering what was happening. "I'd better head off," he told her, slipping his arm out of her grasp. He looked back at Dionne, just a dot in the fields, and wondered if she had drawn the wrong conclusions from what she had just seen.

Amanda squeezed her lips together and fought for courage. Now or never, girl, she encouraged herself. "Do you want to come in?"

"I've got to head back, stuff to do," Jack told her, completely missing the tone in her voice. She looked as though she wanted to tell him something. "It'll wait till Tuesday, won't it?"

"I hardly think it's appropriate for the workplace."

What the hell?

"Look, Jack," she started, beginning to grow a little frustrated that he was being so bloody dense. He was a man of the world, he knew how things worked. She'd heard idle gossips tell of a time when he'd been quite a local feature with the ladies. He must have realised she was inviting him up into her bed. "I appreciate it's not the easiest situation, what with me being your boss, but I really like you and I think…"

"Amanda," he interrupted quickly, jolting back in a panic as he realised what she was saying. "You're a great mate, you know, I like working with you and all that, but…"

"But you're single, aren't you?"

"Yes, but…"

She smiled her most seductive smile at him. "Well then."

"I just don't think of you in that way."

Her smile dropped.

"I'm sorry. You're a mate, I…"

"Leave it," she snapped. Her shoulders slumped, handbag knocking against her knees, loosely held in dejected fingers that had been looking forward to better things. "I don't need to hear all those lines again." She turned and went into her home. Jack was left alone outside.

In the meantime Dionne had made real progress across the fields and was now scrambling down a steep wooded bank. She was glad she'd put her long boots on today – it saved her calves from being scratched by twigs, for this wasn't a regularly used path. Not that she was really thinking about things such as the condition of her skin.

A mad scramble and the path ended at a small estate. Cutting down a thicket, she came out onto the road, and was soon heading around to her flat. She didn't bother paying Mark a visit. Guessing he would be out in the yard, she went around the back of the building and hurried up to her door before he would see her.

Staggering into the shadows of her home, she flicked the lock back and sank against the door, throwing her keys down onto the floorboard. The silence ran up and ate into her. She gazed across the living room. Hardly living. Bare floorboards, no furniture, no pictures on the walls. Shabby curtains to keep up appearances to the outside world. The line of piles of paper on the floor. A line of accusations. A random collection of rough pieces of rock lining the alcove, including the few pieces of rose quartz she had found in the river.

Stupid girl. She should not have listened to the Professor or Mark and their stupid insinuations. Or if she must listen, she shouldn't take them seriously. She bit her lip and told herself she didn't care. Wiped at her eyes with the back of her hand. She didn't care; she honestly didn't care. It had just been nice to think she had something to look forward to. But realistically, she couldn't have anything to look forward to, could she? This was it: her empty flat with the bare essentials; constant work, days flashing by, the weeks and the months. Nothing but working and earning and paying. No change. There was no way out and she certainly didn't want to put herself in a position of having to let anyone know how it really was. Independence and isolation was how it was going to be.

And after what she had done, she really didn't deserve any better.

After a particularly miserable night's sleep, Dionne declared she didn't care whilst glaring at herself in the mirror. The power of suggestion had temporarily set her off kilter, but she was better now. She just needed a day or two to get her inner balance together before she could continue as normal. She rang around and found out about a few house clearance auctions, a little further afield than she usually bothered to go, but she told Hammond Wagstaff that it was worth her spending the day sourcing new second hand material. What she didn't tell him was that she didn't want to be in the bookshop.

Jack had wandered by the bookshop in the afternoon hoping to speak to Dionne. The Professor apologised and explained she was out at auctions for the next two days. It happened sometimes. They shared a bland conversation for five minutes out of politeness before Jack went on his way. The Professor watched him leave and wondered what had happened over the weekend.

Dionne worked shifts at the pub Mondays and Tuesdays. She had been pleasant, exchanged words when he spoke to her, but she was slightly distant, always just needing to do something. Jack didn't usually bother trying to read too much into people's behaviour and he had been told off by ex girlfriends in the past for missing signals – certainly Amanda's seduction attempt on Sunday had been a surprise – but he was a little down that Dionne did appear to be avoiding him.

Amanda had been cool on Tuesday for the matinee. Professional and businesslike but she hadn't wanted to stay too long in his company. She had accounts to deal with, she explained, and closed herself into the office to work in solitude. After all, she had her conference to go to on Wednesday, so she needed to catch up with her work in advance.

Wednesday afternoon found Dionne and the Professor bickering over boxes and boxes of second hand books: where to store them; were they even worth keeping and not just throwing in the recycling bin. Dionne pointed out that she could just take another room upstairs – the first floor that could have been renovated and rented out as a flat if only the Professor could be bothered to do anything about it. Instead Dionne had her stores of second hand surplus books up in what would have been quite a nice living room.

The floor in the back room had vanished and one had to carefully slot feet down into the narrow spaces between boxes to get across to the kettle to make a cup of tea. Dionne was stood at the back of the room, in a green 50s halter neck sun dress, hands on hips, the queen of dusty books. She had a hefty book on the principles of mathematics in one hand like a bomb she was about to lob at the Professor.

"I am not getting rid of a single book," she reiterated. "I will get these all listed online and they will get sold. I will move them upstairs when I've finished."

"It will take forever, Dionne. You can't leave all these boxes in here. One of us is going to break a leg soon."

She rolled her eyes. "We will be fine."

This was how Jack found them at closing time. From the cash desk he had a good view through the open door, past the Professor, over the sea of cardboard boxes to Dionne at the back, illuminated by the window behind.

"You two having fun?"

Simultaneously they both glared in the direction of the question. Neither looked amused.

"You weren't joking when you said she'd gone to buy some books."

The Professor sighed and edged away from the back room. "When it comes to books, I never joke, Mr Dougan." He stepped up to the cash desk and set his hands on the top in the manner of one working in a casino. "Now, is this a book related call or have you come here to see Dionne? I warn you, she is highly irritable this afternoon."

In the background Dionne stomped her foot. "I am not."

"If you wanted to ease the situation you could help her carry the books upstairs."

"No problem."

"No you can't!"

The Professor ignored Dionne and smiled gratefully as Jack came around to the doorway. Dionne was trying to pick her way back through the boxes at speed, still clutching the textbook.

"I haven't listed a single one of these books yet."

"You can sit upstairs and make your lists."

"You want me to sit up there with all the spiders?"

"I'm sure they won't mind. Now, if you'll excuse me, I think I'm going to have a sit down on our very comfortable settee and enjoy a good book."

"You're not going to help?"

"Those books are not my responsibility."

Dionne swore under her breathe. She looked at Jack. No, she was perfectly calm. This was not going to be a problem. "You don't need to do anything," she told him. "I can take these books up myself."

"It's not a problem. There's a lot of books here." He paused, watching her as she gave up and tossed the textbook into one of the open boxes. "You're looking very summery today."

Dionne glanced uncertainly at him, before squatting down to get a grip on one of the boxes. "Yes, well," she huffed as she pushed her fingers under the base. "I needed a bit of a cheer up. Need to convince myself it is summer now." She hoisted the box up and balanced it against her hip like a dumpy overweight baby. "Just grab any box and follow me."

There was another door in the side of the room, thankfully not blocked by boxes, through which was the corridor and staircase up to the first floor. The décor deteriorated rapidly as they ascended – this was the part the Professor had never bothered to decorate. It was a dusty muddled mess, one room stacked with books; paper notes sticking out of piles here and there like flags to help Dionne navigate her way through the storage system.

They didn't say much as they banged their way up and down the stairs with the books. Every time Dionne came down, a little hotter and sweatier than before, she saw the Professor sat comfortably on the settee. What a gentleman. He worked here; he owned the bloody shop. Not only was Jack helping, but he was careful enough to pick out the heaviest boxes and leave the paperbacks for her.

When she'd taken the last box, she nipped through to the toilet and locked the door. She was hot and sweaty. Not that it really mattered, she was only going home, but she quickly wiped down under her armpits and sprayed herself with a cheap can of body spray she left in the cupboard for emergencies. Splashed a little cold water on her face and the back of her neck. Refreshed and calm again, she was ready to leave.

Jack was stood talking to the Professor when she emerged from the back. They stopped talking and looked over at her.

The Professor smiled. "Thank you for that."

Oh, I love smugness, she thought sarcastically as she picked her bag up from under the desk. "I'm going home now. I'll leave you to lock up if that's all right."

"Perfectly acceptable."

Jack followed her out of the shop and onto the street. It was a warm evening, the sun still strong, glowing off her bare shoulders. "You're not going home yet."

Dionne turned to look up at him, the full skirts of her dress swaying dramatically round. "Oh yes I am. I've had enough for today."

"Come on," he said in an easy way, putting an arm around her shoulders to redirect her back into town. "I thought you were wanting a look at the old cells."

"I thought they were locked up."

"They are but we do have keys."

"I thought…" Dionne stopped herself, not sure how to refer to the cinema manager in front of Jack. "I thought your boss said it was a fire risk."

"I think we'll be all right. Besides, she's at a conference."

Curiosity got the better of her. Once she had started on a new subject, she had to follow it through to the end, taking every possibility to glean more information, research it as much as she could. Study it to death. This would probably be the only chance she would get to take a look at the place Saskia Weaver had spent her last night alive.

The temperature dropped noticeably as they passed below ground level, walking down the stone steps to the cellar level. There was an electric lighting system fixed crudely up on the ceiling, giving the noticeably old stone work an artificial glow. There wasn't very much down there – neither storage from the cinema nor remnants of the past. No iron bars or shackles, beds of hay, bones of prisoners long forgotten. There were three side rooms like small alcoves, arched door-sized entrances to each one.

Dionne walked ahead and stepped into the middle one. She looked up at the ceiling, then turned around on the spot. It was earthly cold here, incredibly still. Like preparation for being buried. She looked back at Jack. "There's not much left down here, is there."

He shrugged and leant against the opposing wall. "Just a few boxes of junk from the cinema no one could be bothered to deal with. Pretty grim though. Being locked in down here."

"I guess that was the idea with prisons."

Dionne walked up to the back wall and put a hand on the stone work. Cold, slightly damp, very depressing. Life and people in general could be incredibly grim at times.

"Were you ok the other day?"

"Sorry?" She glanced back at him.

"You were up on the bank, your head between your knees."

It's really none of your business, is it? She thought sourly, looking away from him. "I was fine. Just ran up the bank a bit too quickly," she lied. "Felt a bit woozy."

Her explanation wasn't entirely convincing, but he suspected he had just crossed a line. The atmosphere needed cheering up. "You didn't have as bad an afternoon as I did then. My boss came on to me."

"I don't see why that's so bad. She's pretty enough."

"Yeah, but I don't want to get involved with her."

"Did she threaten you with your job?" Dionne walked out of the cell.

Jack laughed, "No, thank Christ. What a dilemma that would have been."

"I've never been in that one thankfully." But what a thought! What if Hammond did decide to come on to her and blackmail her into an affair if she wanted to keep her job? Dionne wasn't sure what she'd do. Although the notion of Hammond trying to seduce her was comical beyond the posing of a realistic hypothetical scenario.

"I'm going to have to go back up now," she told him. "I'm getting cold down here."

When she reached the lobby she was keen to go home but Jack wouldn't hear of it.

She glanced over the film poster for Wednesday evening as the usher rummaged behind the ticket desk, switching on the lights, getting the sweets out onto the display. "I'm not that fussed about seeing that film."

"Yeah, but you've never seen a film from the projection room, have you." He was determined to spend more time with her, to get her to relax properly with him. "Come on, Dionne, you're interested in random things. Something to try before you die." He grabbed her hand and dragged her up the staircase.

The projection room was an awkward shaped space. Squeezed up at the back of the auditorium, it sat on a higher level in a building that hadn't been erected with cinemas in mind. Boxes and tins of film reel were stacked up at the side on a narrow table. A few rags and tools scattered here and there. It looked like clutter, but Jack probably knew exactly where everything was.

The projector itself was the centre piece and took up most of the dark, windowless room. There were two relatively small squares cut out of the dividing wall: one for the projection to stream out of; a smaller for the projectionist to view the auditorium and the screen ahead. Dionne gazed up at the machine; it looked like a weapon of mass destruction; just swing it around, tilt it back and you could shoot alien invaders out of the sky.

The harsh scrape as he dragged a long metal storage chest across the floor brought her wandering imagination back.

"You can sit on this," he told her. "And watch through there. First class seat."

He was so excited by it all, like a little boy showing off his toys, that Dionne didn't have the heart to tell him she'd rather be in bed. Alone. Asleep. She sat primly on the end of the box and shivered as the chill of the metal went straight through the fabric of her dress and to the back of her legs.

Jack rattled around his tiny empire. He'd done most of the work before he'd come to collect her. He just had the second spool on the projector to spool up with the final section of the film and he'd be ready to roll. He took the lid off one of the canisters; muttering to himself, opening up the projector. At one point he found an old fleece he had worn to work once and forgotten to take home again, casually dropping it over her shoulders as he shuffled by. Dionne sat and listened to the hushed conversations as the patrons filed in. Watched Jack fit the last of film into the projector, his tongue sticking out of the corner of his mouth in concentration. He glanced up and winked at her. "Got to make sure the adverts get shown all right." It wasn't the adverts he was putting in, but she wasn't to know that.

"How long have you been working here?"

"About four years." Something snapped shut.

Four years, Dionne thought, looking back out of the window as the adverts started. Longer than she had lived in this little town. He would have been in here, tinkering with the projector, when she had moved in.

The lights in the auditorium went down a notch further as the main feature made ready its entrance. She felt that expectation she always got in a cinema when the film was about to begin. A hush fell in the auditorium. Jack was still busy with the film. The room was darker now, Jack lit up by the bulb in the projector. Abruptly he had finished, and dropped onto the steel box next to her, leaning forward to peer through the hole in the wall to make sure everything was running correctly. She could feel his body against the length of her – there was only just enough space for them both to sit on the box – the musky smell of aftershave and sweat. The fleece being pressed against the side of her bare arm. His shoulder slipped behind hers so they fitted more snugly on the box.

If she was honest, the film was better than she had been expecting. She had written it off as something that wasn't for her when she had read the reviews in the newspaper. It was never going to be a favourite, but it could pass a couple of hours. Although she could never really loose herself in it, all the time very conscious of Jack being right beside her. He got up part way through the film to manually switch over to the second spool on the projector, but apart from those few minutes he was always there. And when that wasn't distracting her, there was always the strange view, like watching the film down the length of a telescope.

The film finished; the credits started to roll. The lights in the auditorium went up half way, people rustling to leave. Dionne smiled to herself; he had been right, it was something you had to try. Watching a film from a projection room. You had to try anything once.

She twisted around to say something to him, to thank him for dragging her up here and persevering. She had forgotten just how close they were sitting, that and the fact that he must have leaned in to whisper something in her ear meant that it was a near miss knocking each other out.

And she forgot what she was going to say. Forgot herself. Felt a knot tie itself up deep inside her chest. An overwhelming urge to push herself onto him. It had been a while since she had been with anyone. She was dizzy. Jack was staring at her mouth.

The door opened fast and unapologetic. Dionne jumped to her feet, turning, seeing Amanda, seeing the look on her face and wishing there was another way out of this room.

Amanda was choking on words. Jack turned around, distinctly irritated. Dionne picked up her bag. "I have to go now," she announced, looking guilty of things she hadn't done. "Thanks, Jack." She hurried past Amanda and down the stairs. Making her cowardly retreat out of there.

Thankful the witch was gone, Amanda slammed the door shut. "What was she doing here?"

An evening so full of promise had really, drastically and terribly gone down hill. Jack wanted to head after Dionne, but he could see Amanda was begging for a fight and wasn't going to let him be until she'd had it. "Watching a film."

"Right, and she couldn't sit in the auditorium with everyone else?"

"If you're worried about the revenue, please take the price of a ticket out of my salary."

"Don't get smart, Jack." Amanda could have hit him. First he rejected her, and now he had to bring that thing up here to flaunt the fact that she had been turned down. He had been hoping she wasn't going to bother coming back to the cinema after her conference at all today. Presuming that while the boss was away, he could do what he liked. He was abusing the fact that he knew she had feelings for him, she told herself. She was going to remind him just who she was. "I suppose you went down to the cellar. You were saying she was interested in that."

Jack muttered something under his breath inaudible to Amanda, swinging up from the box.

"I know you went down there. Mary said she saw you two come out from there."

"Don't start this, Amanda."

"Don't tell me what to do," she shrieked, no longer worried whether anyone was still in the auditorium listening. "I'm the boss. I told you I wanted no one down there. You knew that."

He held up his hands. "All right, I shouldn't have done that. I didn't see what harm it would do." He passed her the key.

"Didn't think? You just wanted to impress that witch."

"Don't say that."

"I'll say what I want. You will do as you're told."

She was starting to look as though she were ready to pop. Jack had never seen Amanda loose her temper in quite this style. He wasn't feeling overly sympathetic however, and didn't appreciate being spoken to like an irresponsible child. "I don't care who you are; you don't speak to me in that tone of voice."

"I'll speak to you in whatever tone I feel like."

"You will be a civilised adult when you speak to me."

She was so mad she wanted to claw his eyes out. Her hands were shaking. She threw the key to the floor. "I don't like being talked to like this by my staff. You're in a lot of trouble."

It was badly timed, but he couldn't help himself: he laughed. She sounded just like his mother now. "Do you want to add a 'young man' to the end of that?"

Her eyes blazed. "You're suspended!"

He let out a deep sigh. She was completely loosing the plot. "Fine, Amanda. You get on there and project your fucking films."

He pushed past her and headed down the staircase. Amanda was stunned. For a moment she stood – thinking and doing nothing. Then she coughed and sat down on the box. It was shocking how that had escalated. Now she had suspended him, and for what? Because he had brought a woman here who he obviously liked in the way she wished he liked her.

Amanda squeezed her eyes shut and swore loudly. And now she really was going to have to project the fucking films.

It had been a particularly quiet Friday afternoon. Quiet to the point of needing to check whether time still actually moved. And because Hammond was out, she had to stay on the shop floor in case anyone did want to buy a book. There were stacks of second hand books upstairs still to be listed, but they would just have to wait.

Dionne was sitting on a stool behind the desk; the sound of her sandal heel clicking against the metal bar footrest the only sound. She had her notebook on Saskia Weaver in front of her, and was reading through her notes. It was growing increasingly frustrating: the question of Andrew Holburn. A man religious to his science. What could he have possibly seen to convince him that Saskia had been able to evoke the dead?

The door went and she looked up from her notes. Jack had turned up, not looking like his usual cheery self. She hadn't seen or heard from him since Wednesday night in the cinema. He was probably angry with her for running out at the first sign of trouble. Coward that she was.

He nodded to her as if they were just passing on the street.

Dionne put her pen down. "You all right?"

"Yeah. You?"

"Fine." This was ridiculous. He was behaving as though there was no reason on earth for him to be here. "Look, I'm sorry I didn't stay to fight your corner the other night."

Jack waved it off. "Wasn't a problem." In truth it was probably a blessing. He wouldn't have wanted anyone else to have heard that overblown telling off.

"Was your boss all right?"

He approached, leaning up against the desk and peering down at Dionne's scribbles. Still messing on with that bloody dead woman. "She went on a bit of a wobbler."

"A bit of a wobbler?"

"She's suspended me."

"What?"

He looked up at her. Straight in the eye.

"I'm really sorry, Jack. I feel awful."

"And you shouldn't. It's not your fault. You didn't even want to sit up there with me…"

"Now, I wasn't…"

"And it wasn't a problem or against company rules or any of that bollocks," he continued, ignoring her attempt at protest. "Amanda went off at the deep end and overreacted big style. I'll leave her to stew over the weekend then see where I stand."

"Maybe you should let her seduce you," Dionne joked awkwardly. "You'd get your job back quicker."

Jack sniffed a humourless laugh. "Yeah," he said, avoiding her gaze.

"Good afternoon, you two." The Professor burst in through the door. "Alan not here yet?"

Dionne raised her eyebrows questioningly. "I wasn't aware he was supposed to be."

"Oh yes, he should be here by now."

As if on cue, Alan stumbled in through the door, slamming it behind him. Panting like a wild dog, his slender rib cage heaving violently with the lungfuls of air he drew inwards. Pale, sweaty features. A bloody nose; an eye rapidly disappearing into puffing skin that was going to turn into a beautiful black eye. His teeth looked to be rimmed with blood, a smear trailing away from his mouth where he had wiped it with the back of his hand. His T-shirt was ripped, his clothes dusty.

The Professor, Dionne and Jack stared back at him in stunted surprise.

Wagstaff was the first to break the silence. "What on earth happened to you?"

"Beat up," Alan coughed.

Dionne could feel apprehensive nausea.

"By who? Why?" The Professor approached his young protégée. "What on earth is going on?"

"Brothers," Alan said, as if that would be enough of an explanation. He saw Dionne close her eyes miserably in the background. She knew what he was talking about. "They said I did it."

"Did what? Do you mean those brothers who came to find that man's killer?"

"They said I'm a freak."

They were interrupted by the sound of furious roars from outside the shop. The Professor looked at Alan. "They chased you here?"

The words became audible. Closer. Alan bolted. The Professor ran for the entrance as the brothers appeared through the windows. Slamming the door to, he pushed the bolts across. The brothers –

angry, sweating bulls, drunk and irrational, shook on the doors, screaming for the murdering freak. That man from the quarry was in the background, egging them on.

"They can't go round lynching innocent people!" Dionne started. Alan pushed past her, stinking of terror, and disappeared into the back room. "What are we supposed to do, barricade ourselves in?"

"Let us at him!"

"Look." She pointed out at the window as she hurried around the cash desk and towards the windows at the front of the shop. "There's that arsehole Seger. He needs to sort this out." She hammered on the window to get his attention. He was on the other side of the high street, casually walking along. He must have already noticed − who could have not reacted to the shouting. He saw Dionne and waved.

She looked desperately into the shop. "He waved at me," she said in disbelief.

A stone came through the window. Dionne screamed, instinctively dropping to a squat and covering her head with her arms. Jack pulled her back into the depths of the shop, watching as the brothers left the door and moved down to the broken window. The intention appeared to be to kick down the remaining glass and charge the shop. "I'll go out and deal with them," he said, passing Dionne to the Professor as he headed determinedly to the door.

"No!" Dionne grabbed for his arm but missed. She and Hammond went after him, like surreal parents terrified for a son about to set out in the real world with no idea of how cruel it really could be.

"You can't reason with people like this," Hammond tried to stop him.

Jack opened the door and stepped out into the breach. The brothers had seen him coming, and had decided not to bother with smashing down what remained of the window. They met Jack on the pavement; no idea who he was or what he had to do with anything.

"Let us in at that little freak, mate."

"He's a fucking murderer."

The stench of alcohol could put you off drinking for life. Jack immediately felt out of his depth. He wasn't a negotiator, a macho man, a fighter or anyone else who might be handy in this kind of situation. He was an odd little nerd trapped in a misleading body who liked to run his historical periodical, build scale models and mess about with the local cinema's antiquated projection system. But once you'd thrown yourself in among the wolves you couldn't let them know you didn't know how to tame them. "You need to go home and sleep this off."

Dionne felt ill. "I can't watch this," she mumbled, turning away from the window she had only been daring to watch from over Hammond's shoulder. She hurried away to the back room, telling herself she was going to check on Alan. She found him blubbering like a two year old on the old settee. As she stepped into the doorway, he looked up and glared at her as if she were personally responsible.

"Get out of here!" he screeched, his voice breaking, tearing apart. She staggered back as he got up and slammed the door that was never shut in her face.

PC Sam Seger had joined the fray at this point. Whether it was out of call of duty or a fear that complaints would be made about him and his inaction was impossible to say. One of the brothers swung a slow punch at Jack, who quite easily ducked out of the way. Seger pulled the brother's arm down.

"You lads need to be heading home."

"There's a fucking murderer in there. A freak."

"And if there is, it's my job to deal with it." Seger held up a hand, surprised by just what a subduing effect he had on them. The man from the quarry was skulking away already. The brothers' fury seemed to be spent. "Go back to your digs and sleep this off, all right?"

One of the brothers pointed at him. "Make sure you sort it."

Having put their point across, they started to disperse. Seger opened the door and entered the now gloomy bookshop. Jack followed him inside.

"Aren't you going to arrest those thugs?" Wagstaff demanded furiously. "Look what they've done. I'm going to be pressing charges, and I am sure Alan will as well."

"What for?"

"Physical assault."

"Grievous bodily harm," Dionne added, staring at Seger with little trust.

Alan: the scrawny little runt that was good for nothing, Seger thought as he glanced over at the broken window. All of this over Alan. It was ridiculous. He looked at Dionne. Jesus, she was another case. If she hadn't such attitude problems he would have taken her out a long time ago. And he hated her for feelings that she brought out of him. "Now, why would they want to attack Alan of all people?"

"Spineless gossips always prey on the weak and the different." Wagstaff was furious. Seger was behaving as if they were in the wrong. He had seen that performance. How could he act as if he wanted to side with the brothers? "There's been a lot of gossip and exaggeration about this murder because the police haven't offered people anything concrete."

"All right, get off your high horse, Doctor."

"Professor. You leave them with nothing and they're frightened and angry and you get a few nasty minds stirring in slander about unpopular people and suddenly you've got yourself a lynch mob." The Professor slammed his fist on the desk. "The police must deal with this. Come down heavy and let them know it will not be tolerated. We are a civilised society."

Seger gave him a withering look. "Where's Alan?"

"In the back room." Dionne stepped away from the desk.

Sighing, thinking that he could do without this, Seger pushed open the door and looked into the room. Alan was sat on the settee shaking. He looked properly beaten. There wasn't really any other angle to put on this. He was going to have to process this incident properly, and go back to the brothers and press charges. This wasn't going to look good in the papers. "Sit tight," he told Alan, "I'm going to call a doctor. I'll need a statement."

He turned back into the bookshop to speak to the others. He wondered why that jogger was here, the man who had been in the park the night Trevor Washington had been murdered. As was Dionne who had been panning in the river, and Wagstaff who had been messing about with lampposts nearby. Was this a bloody conspiracy? He glanced down at the desk. There was an open A4 notepad with hand written notes. He saw the name Saskia Weaver.

"Who's Saskia Weaver?"

"What?" The Professor sounded disgusted.

"That has nothing to do with anything," Dionne snapped, reaching for her notepad. "Don't go poking through my things."

"This is a crime scene."

"Do you always have to be an arsehole?" She picked up the book and snapped it shut.

There was the attitude again. "She might be relevant."

"I hardly think so. She died over two hundred years ago. The last witch to be executed in this town."

Seger stared at her for a little longer than was necessary. Witches now? He thought silently in amusement. "I need to use your phone, *Professor*," he started, still looking at Dionne. "I need to get a doctor down here and someone to take a look at that window. You don't mind, do you?"

"Be my guest."

The aftermath of Alan's beating was a continued escalation of tensions. On the day of the assault the gathering in the bookshop grew: the usual suspects, the doctor, the ever popular Seger and a couple of his colleagues to help with the crime scene. Collecting the evidence, taking statements and generally looking bored, whilst Seger and the doctor dealt with Alan. The Professor ran in circles through the bookshop, ranting about his rights. He was going to press charges. Thugs like that should not be allowed to get away with bully-boy behaviour.

Then Seger and the doctor came through from the back room and announced that Alan was not going to press charges.

They had been horrified. Alan walked out before them, a stitch in his eyebrow, his face mashed and puffed but now washed. Dry eyed, cold looking, trying to be brave, quivering with fear in the depths. He said he wanted this to end now. The Professor ran after him, calling him a fool, telling him there was no reason to be afraid anymore.

Alan didn't change his mind. He hid in his parents' house; didn't turn up for work on Monday. Sent his resignation in a letter of uncertainly formed letters, staggering into a new and terrifying world. He wouldn't speak to anyone.

All the police could do was charge one of the brothers with destruction of private property. The brothers paid for the repairs on the shop window. Jack helped the Professor nail up a piece of chipboard over the gap as a temporary measure. After the weekend Dionne was glad of the shield.

This drama had been watched by a lot of bystanders, and people will gossip. The whole town knew by Saturday morning. Word leached out to the wider world, and the newspaper men landed once again in the little market town. The plot thickened. There was nothing more substantial about the murder of Trevor Washington, but in its place they had sensation and soap opera. The cameras hounded the brothers; waited outside Alan's home, calling from mobile phones, desperate for an interview. They took photographs of the bookshop with the boarded up window. Came inside and pestered Dionne to the point of irritation that she locked the door and refused to let anyone in.

The ongoing saga was back on the front of the local papers again. The brothers appeared on the local news' evening television broadcast. Shouting about their brother, mumbling that the 'incident' may have been a mistake. But as Alan continued his strike of silence and refused to press charges, there were some who wondered if there was something in it. The mere suggestion that it could have been a local made people more suspicious of one another. It was not such a friendly town anymore. Dionne buried herself deeper into her work and her books.

On Monday Amanda had turned up at Jack's home to apologise. She hoped they could put all their awkwardness and misunderstandings behind them. She hoped Jack would return with immediate effect and be ready for the Tuesday matinee. The weekend had not gone well. Amanda had tried with the projector, but the angrier she got the less the machine wanted to cooperate. In the end she had been forced to persuade a friend of the previous projectionist (now deceased) to come in and help because she was desperate and hadn't dared call Jack after what had happened.

Of course it was flattering to hear you were indispensible, but it made Jack think about the position of the cinema. If there was only him and an old local nearing ninety who could work the projector, either they needed a new projector – which the cinema really couldn't afford at the moment – or he needed to train someone else how to use it. He wasn't intending on leaving the cinema any time soon, but what if he went on a holiday, was sick or moved away?

He pondered over the matter on his walk home from the cinema one early Sunday evening. Turning the corner, he was surprised to see Dionne perched on his doorstep, clutching a large brown paper parcel and reading a paperback book.

She looked up as he approached, slipping a torn piece of newspaper into the book as a marker. "I was beginning to wonder if you'd ever come home. The film did finish at quarter to five."

He smiled, wondering just how long she had been waiting. "I had to tidy round a bit before I could go."

"I would have thought your boss would still be grovelling and doing your tidying up for you," Dionne commented idly as she stood up.

"If you're going to be mates again you can't keep rubbing the other fella's nose in it once you've said you'll let them off."

"I suppose." She watched as he unlocked the front door.

Jack paused and looked over at her. "I don't think you've ever been over to my place before."

"That's because you've never asked," Dionne answered primly. "Besides, I'm here in an official capacity." She patted the parcel she was holding. "This is for you."

"Well, you'd better come in then."

Jack wandered straight through the living room to the kitchen at the back of the building. Dionne took her time. As he had pointed out, she had never been here before. She was curious about what the house of Jack would look like. Photographs of Jack on a clipper ship, windswept and rugged. A picture of a family, two sons, both with his resemblance, one rather chubby. Dionne peered closely at it. Was that Jack as a youth?

She stepped back and gazed up at the lines of tiny model ships on the shelving around the top of the living room. It looked as though every tiny detail had been faithfully recorded. "Did you make these?" She asked, her neck craned back.

Jack glanced through the doorway. "Yeah."

"Are they to scale?"

Out in the kitchen, Jack chuckled to himself. "Yes."

When there were no more questions, he went to the living room to check she hadn't snuck out the front door, worried about consorting with an oddity. She was stood in front of a large map of Australia on the wall. Still here. "Are you going to give me my parcel?"

"Oh, yes, of course." She hurried over to the kitchen, passing the parcel. "It's from my dad, although you probably already guessed that. He was up yesterday."

"Finished already?"

"Yes." Dionne sat down at the kitchen table and stared at a bag of apples.

Jack set the parcel on the kitchen table and carefully unwrapped it. Inside, neatly folded in tissue paper, was a suit. He pulled out the jacket, holding it up for inspection. "You can tell your old man I'm impressed."

"Are those apples good?"

"What?" He got the impression he was talking to himself. Dionne was staring at a bag of apples he'd bought the other day. "Probably," he answered, a little distracted. "I haven't had one yet."

"Can I have one?" She looked up at him, wide-eyed innocence. "I wouldn't normally be so cheeky you understand, it's just that I'm starving."

"Sure, help yourself." He put the jacket down and leant against the kitchen worktop. Watching as Dionne tore the plastic bag with a finger nail, taking an apple out and biting into it. "You know how Alan's doing?"

She shook her head, chewing and swallowing. "Hammond's been trying to get to speak to him all week but his mother says he's refusing to see anyone. He's handed his notice in at the quarry."

"Still not pressing charges?"

"It's worrying. I'm sure Alan didn't kill that guy, but I don't know why he doesn't press charges. Those meat heads are getting away with murder."

"Not literally."

"Well, no, not literally," she conceded. "But even so, they shouldn't be allowed to behave like that. They've already paid for the damage at the shop at least. We're getting the new window fitted on Monday."

"You still getting bothered by the journalists?"

"They seem to have given up. Touch wood." She tapped the table.

Jack watched as she finished the apple, barely a scrap of flesh remaining as she set the core primly on the table. She looked up at him, a little embarrassed by his attention. "Thank you for that."

"No problem. You want to stay for dinner?"

"Oh, I couldn't," she said. Her stomach irritably announced they could most definitely stay and get a proper meal.

"Yeah you can. Nothing fancy."

"All right." She paused, thinking, looking through the door. "You've got a television? Mind if I catch the news?"

She made it sound as though few people had televisions. Jack waved at the living room. "Be my guest."

The quiet sound of the television accompanied him as he cooked. When he went through to invite her to eat, she was fast asleep on the settee, curled up underneath the fleece jacket from the cinema he'd picked up earlier in the week.

Dionne stood and stared out of the new pane of glass in the bookshop. The minor refurbishment wasn't tempting anyone to come in. She glanced at her watch. Thursday late nights were awful if people didn't come in. And she still had a shift to do at the pub before she could call it a night.

The Professor wasn't here to keep her company. He had said something about an appointment and that he wouldn't be in all day. Looked as though he already was elsewhere as he informed her. Driven off to somewhere else and left her to man the ship alone.

Maybe she could lock up before seven. It seemed pointless hanging around when no one was going to come in and buy any thing.

Picking up a small stack of books that needed shelving, she wandered through to the side room at the end: through the archway and into the annex. She stared at the books already on the shelf and shivered. It was dull and dark today: the clouds a tight old crew, the drizzle pounding softly down and the damp chill creeping through the building. She was in her woollen jumper dress but felt as though she were standing in thin, wet clothes.

She was just feeling disgruntled, unsettled. A little sunshine and she would be all right, she said to herself. Shifting the weight of the books to one arm, she reached out with her right hand to make a space between two hardback books on the shelf. And felt as though she were being watched.

Outside the drizzle gently pattered and ran down the window. The stone buildings of the high street were an array of wet greys, half-hidden in the murky evening light. Jack was on the pavement outside, hands in his jacket; damp, flattened hair from the rain. A strange expression on his face that she couldn't quite place. He stood and watched her, not reacting when she turned her head and met his gaze. An old sensation swept up through her body, a warming notion, and Dionne forgot herself. She didn't wave, smile or make any action towards him. It didn't seem necessary from either side of the glass division. Just the intensity of stopping and looking at one another; being there.

One of the books slipped out of the pile she was holding, slowly at first before a sky dive down to the floor. It hit her foot, making her wince. She drew her foot back and crouched down to pick up the book. When she looked back at the window Jack had gone. Maybe he had never even been there. She walked to the window to see if he had just started walking up the street again. He wasn't anywhere. Maybe it was just her imagination. She'd spent most of the day on her own not talking to or seeing anyone. In desperation she was hallucinating friends.

Turning away, she went back to the bookshelf and found Jack stood in the archway. Droplets of rain caught on his jacket. The cuffs of his trousers wet from splashing through puddles. A trickle of rainwater running down past his eye.

"Oh." Dionne was surprised by his sudden reappearance. He still didn't say anything. It was growing increasingly dreamlike, surreal. He stepped down into the annex room. Staring into her. He was right in front of her, in her personal space, in her breathing air. The temperature rose. She didn't know quite what to do with herself. "I…" she started as the books fell from her arm.

Jack took her face and kissed her. Dionne staggered back, soon up against the bookshelf. She had convinced herself that she was not interested, but the dam had been released and it was all rushing out. She had handfuls of his jacket, pulling him to her against the bookshelf, kissing him back. Her mind was a whirr. She'd forgotten they were in front of the side window for all passer bys to see. She'd forgotten she was at work. A lit-up side show in darkness. She just knew that right now he was up against her and she wanted him.

The bell went upon the opening of the door. She opened her eyes, focusing on the books coming at her from all directions and realising a customer must have entered the shop. She drew her lips away from his, trying to wriggle free of his embrace. "There's someone in the shop."

He ran a hand down her arm. "You'll be shutting the shop soon."

"I have a shift at the pub."

He looked distinctly irritated, pulling away from her.

"Excuse me!" A shrill female voice called from the front of the shop.

Dionne could have screamed. She didn't want this to finish barely after the starting line.

Jack gave her a nudge to the archway. "I'll see you at the pub then."

"Promise?"

"Of course."

Dionne's guide to men – part three

Don't.

It might be exciting in the first heart-fluttering moments, but after that they are going to want to know about you. They may not want to sit and discuss feelings, but one way or another, they will find out things. They'll want to go back to your home. They'll want access to your secrets, to you. Poke their way into your privacy. They want to be inside you. Literally and metaphorically speaking.

Dionne understood that circumstances dictated she had to be independent and alone. She should not have allowed it to happen. She felt she had to end it all, despite her misgivings.

It was Friday morning; she was sitting at Jack's kitchen table and was convinced she was about to throw up. It was never nice doing these things, especially when part of you wanted to cling on. She had to be strong.

She had looked at herself in the bathroom mirror this morning. The old worry was showing in her face again. She'd pulled her clothes on and padded downstairs, cursing her stupidity and trying to think of the best words to say to deal with this mess.

Jack cheerily wandered into the kitchen, kissing the top of her head as he went by. "Morning. You off to work soon?"

Dionne stared out of the window. She wanted to cry. "Yes."

Jack was filling the kettle at the tap. "Can I see you again tonight? I can come over to your place."

The very suggestion made her stomach turn. "No."

"All right." He turned off the tap, glancing back at her, a little surprised by the monosyllabic answers. Perhaps Dionne wasn't a morning person. "You can come over here."

"No."

"No? Are you busy?"

She squeezed her eyes shut. "Look, Jack, there's no easy way to say this. Last night was a mistake. I shouldn't have let myself get carried away."

He carefully put the kettle down on the kitchen worktop. Dionne couldn't tell if he was angry or upset.

"Carried away?"

"I don't want to discuss it," she said, standing up from the kitchen table. "But this is over before it starts. I'd appreciate it if you stayed away from me."

He'd turned around. "What the hell are you talking about?"

"I have to go to work."

"You're not walking out on me now."

He reached forward as if to pull her to him. "No!" Dionne shouted, jumping out of reach. "Don't touch me. Don't speak to me. That's it. I want nothing to do with you." She hurried out of his house, slamming the door behind her. She hadn't phrased that quite right; what she had meant to say was that she didn't want him having anything to do with her. She hadn't meant to sound as thought she was disgusted by him. The end result was the same though, and she'd left him with no ambiguity. That ought to be the end of it.

Except that it wasn't. At least not for her.

What had been drizzle turned into full bloodied rain. It was blown down from the hills, thrashing relentlessly onto the little Dales town. People avoided going outside as much as possible, hunched figures running from doorway to doorway. Windscreen wipers repetitively sliding across car windows, depressed expressions staring out onto the road.

Dionne had arrived for work in time but in a foul mood. Judging by the look on her face, it was best to pretend he hadn't even noticed, the Professor surmised. At first he put it down to the weather, but two hours and many cups of tea and biscuits later, she was still slumped on that stool by the desk, miserable, as if the life had been drained out of her. Her fingers drummed on the desk in time with the rain. A man came in and asked about a book. He had to ask his question twice before Dionne even realised he was there.

The post arrived. The Professor Wagstaff accepted the delivery, flicking through the uninspiring collection of letters, bills and advertisers.

"And yet more letters trying to persuade me to take a company credit card," he grumbled, ripping the circular in two without even taking the paper out of the envelope. "I have a friend who is interested in these things, in economics," he started as he ambled up to the window to survey the rain. "He says this is going to come back and haunt us soon." He looked at the clouds, at the sky. This would clear by the late afternoon.

He looked back at Dionne who did not look as though she was really concentrating.

"Credit cards," he said loudly.

Dionne visibly jumped at the volume, shaken by the mention of the word.

"People living on credit, building up thousands and thousands in debt. People with overloaded house loans. People spending more than they have. My friend says this bubble is getting ready to burst."

She looked disturbed.

"It's all down to the greed of people. Oh, certainly not the likes of you and I." He looked around and was surprised to see Dionne's hand unconsciously balling up into a fist. She really didn't want small talk today.

"Accounts," he burst out. "I have to work on the accounts. I can't be disturbed. You can man the ship on your own, can't you?"

Man the ship. The ship. Ship. Ships to scale. Naval and seafaring history. Jack. Dionne felt sick. Hammond walked by into the back room, closing the seldom-closed door. She shouldn't be taking all of this out on him, but she couldn't even bear speaking at the moment. Thinking was torture enough.

Her mind was stuck in last night. Granted, it had been a long time, and a man dying of thirst will probably be grateful of a glass of urine if it comes down to it. But it had been good. Her thoughts ambled down the lines of her memories, waving happy, heart-fluttering moments in her path, sending her stumbling back. She'd pause to catch her breath again and could feel his warm hands on her skin. Being that energetic, that wanting. Breathing in his scent. Breathlessness. Sweat beads. Her hair brushing against her naked back as she craned her head backwards. Those ripples of incredible sensation pumping up through her body.

The rain drummed against the windows. Then she thought about her flat. About how she couldn't let it go forward.

But surely she could have worked something out. She was intelligent enough. Cunning. Inventive. After everything she had done, all that she had achieved, ploughing on where most would have been too scared of life. And to trip up over this little thing? At the end of the day, were her problems even important in the grand schemes of life?

She though about the sensation of his mouth on her throat.

She had been an idiot. Panic could do that to a person.

Fear bit into her stomach. She had just tossed away the one good thing she had found in a long time. Why? Nervousness crept upon her. She needed to settle this. But it was only eleven in the morning and she didn't finish until five. She had to let him know that she hadn't meant what she said.

Glancing furtively, she picked up the phone and listened to it ring. She didn't know what she was going to say, especially in a bookshop, but she had to catch him before he took her at her word and never saw her again. He'd be upset, look for comfort somewhere. Go to the cinema, old trustworthy cinema, and see that woman, the cinema manager. She'd comfort him and reassure him he was a catch. They'd be married before the month was out.

Dionne's hand was shaking.

He didn't pick up the call. It went to answer phone. Dionne hung up. He had to be at home. He wasn't working at the cinema – there were no films screened on a Friday – and he had said something about needing to do work on the periodical. He had to be at home. Maybe he was a little upset, but he would still have to answer the phone. That call could have been about his bloody stupid magazine for all he knew.

He could have just been in the bathroom. She'd give him ten minutes then try again.

She rang after six minutes. Another half hour. An hour. No reply. The phone rang and rang and went to answer phone.

He's ignoring me, Dionne told herself as she pulled on her trench coat and went to tell Hammond she was going out for lunch.

The Professor glanced out of the window, and then gave her a curious look. These were the first words she had said to him this morning. He pointed at the coat hooks. "There's an umbrella there you can borrow."

Dionne took the umbrella, but with the wind blowing the rain and her distraction, the umbrella blew inside out three times before she gave up. Closing it, she carried it like an offensive weapon, threatening it at any pedestrians who would dare try and slow her down on the pavement.

She got to his house and was relieved to see the car on the drive. He hadn't left town. She ran up to the building and hammered on the front door. Waited for the sound of eager footsteps that did not come. Hammered again. Went back to the road to gaze up at the building. There were no lights on and no obvious signs of anyone peering out of the windows. She returned to the house and tried the front door. It was locked. She peered in through the front window. Empty. She marched into the back garden, looking in all the windows, shaking the back door to try and get in. Everything was locked and it looked as though he was not home.

Where was he?

She walked back past the cinema. It was locked up and dark. If it weren't for the fact that his boss had made a pass at him, she might have drummed her fists on the door and begged the woman to tell her where he was. Appealed to the sisterhood or some such thing that people liked to think was inherent in all.

Dionne hurried and went back to work.

The Professor peered out of the office as the door went. Dionne looked drenched and desperate. Her hair was plastered to her scalp, hanging down like long black rats' tails. She took off her coat and raindrops scattered to the carpet.

"Umbrella not much use on a day like this?"

"No," she mumbled, unaware of her state. Thoughtlessly, she set the wet umbrella on the desk. The Professor carefully picked up the offending article and took it through to the sink.

"You should dry yourself up," he told her.

"Yes," she said quietly, going through to the bathroom. She stood in front of the mirror, the raindrops having mixed with her eye shadow. It looked as though she had been crying. She tore off some toilet paper and cleaned up her eyes. Why was she behaving like this, so desperately? Have a little dignity. This pathetic neediness is beneath you. She reapplied mascara and returned to the shop.

At three in the afternoon she found the courage to leave a halting and awkward message on the answer phone.

He didn't call back.

At five o'clock, the rain had eased off into light drizzle, the last drabs before it dried up completely. Dionne left the bookshop promptly and went back to Jack's house. He wasn't at home. Or if he was, he was hiding upstairs and ignoring her. Where could he be?

Perhaps he had gone for a jog. He liked jogging. He would be angry about what she had said. Needed to clear his head. That was the explanation, Dionne convinced herself. He was probably in the park – she had seen him jogging there before.

She wandered every track in the park and surroundings, desperately looking at every jogger who was venturing out after the rain. Her shoes got muddy from trekking up and down the more minor routes through rain sodden grass. She paused at a shallow point in the stream to wash off the soles of her shoes. She gazed up the bank, to the path to the folly. The police had opened up the area again. You were allowed to go up there, but from what she had heard people still avoided the place. Jack wouldn't be up there. She didn't want to go and check.

Shivering, she turned away. Besides, he would have jogged down from there by now and she would have seen him somewhere in the park.

She went to the *Blacksmith's Anvil*, hoping he had forgotten that she did not work Fridays. Jack wouldn't give up on her that easily. Mark was having a quick pint before heading home to finish a commission for delivery tomorrow.

"Not looking your best, Dionne," he commented as she peered in the bar, looking across the clientele for someone who was not there.

She thought about her scruffy hair, her damp coat and her mud stained shoes. "It's the weather."

"Oh right." Mark drained the last of his pint. "You looking for someone?"

She looked him straight in the eye, for the first time paying proper attention. "Jack's not been in?"

Mark shook his head. "Not whilst I've been here."

"I've got to go."

He was definitely avoiding her. But he had not left the town because his car was here. He was drowning his sorrows, she decided. There were other pubs in town, and obviously he wouldn't go to the *Blacksmith's* because that was where she worked. He would have thought to himself: she doesn't work Fridays, but I don't want to risk it. She made a careful tour of the pubs in town, but did not find him.

She finished at the base of the hill, at the top of which was the cinema manager's cottage. It was the only other place Dionne could think he might be. The one place she couldn't check. She could hardly go up there, knock on the door, get them out of bed and demand that he let her explain herself. Explain why she didn't want him to see where she lived, what really happened in her life.

Dionne squeezed her lips together and felt liquid that she told herself was a raindrop slide down her cheek. She'd really managed to screw this one up in style. Record timing. Some people obviously weren't meant to cope with relationships. Think positive, she told herself weakly. Your secret is safe and the status quo may continue long into the future. This is for the best.

She walked home slowly, working through the arguments as to why this had worked out the best way. Her gut instinct this morning had been the right one. Get rid of him, make it clear you don't want him in your life. This hole is of my own making and there's only room for one.

She reached her home turf. The light was fading rapidly. Dusk was falling. End of the day. Game over. Light came through Mark's kitchen window onto his work yard. Furniture was under a tarpaulin. He must have finished in time for tomorrow. A couple of mugs of cold, drunk tea were still on the workbench. Hard at it all evening. Whilst she'd been running about town like an idiot.

She fumbled for her keys in her pocket and walked up to the door. Put the key in the lock and twisted it. The lock released, the door was ready, but she didn't open it. She didn't really want to go in. Back to that life she wasn't going to escape.

And that was when it happened.

"I was beginning to wonder when you were coming home."

A sensation flooded through and suddenly she felt tired. There was something reassuring in the tone of that voice with its Australian twang that allowed her to relax. She hung onto the key as if the strength in her knees might give way any moment.

Jack leant nonchantly against the wall a little further down from her door as if he did this all the time. "So where've you been?"

"Around town." Her stomach felt nervous. Maybe this wasn't all settled just yet.

"Mark said you'd been in the *Blacksmith's*"

"You were there?"

"Nah." He shook his head. "I was here, talking to your neighbour."

Dionne thought back to those two mugs of tea on the workbench and of how Mark could talk. She wondered just how much those two had talked.

"So am I all right to be talking to you now?"

She smiled tightly and looked down at her feet. She felt embarrassed thinking how she had overreacted and panicked this morning. It wasn't something she could explain easily. "I... I wasn't quite thinking this morning."

"You looked like you were having some kind of nervous attack."

She didn't know what to say to that.

"So can I come in?"

This was the point of no return. Once he walked through that door, he would know. Even if she didn't explain, he was intelligent enough to work it out for himself. He would know. He might not like her in the new light. It might be the end. On the other hand, she could end it now by shutting the door in his face.

Dionne pulled the door open. "Sure," she said quietly.

He had been curious about where Dionne lived for a long time. He'd imagined all kinds of settings, but this had never come up in the string of imagined dwellings. Jack slowed in the middle of the room as the door swung shut, his footsteps echoing on the floor in the empty room. Empty. No furniture of any description. Shabby curtains, piles of papers on the floor and some assorted rocks on an inbuilt shelf. There wasn't even a lampshade on the naked bulb hanging from the ceiling. He didn't quite know what to say. "You lived here long?"

"About three years." Dionne went to the bathroom to hang up her wet coat.

Jack looked uncomfortable. He had realised something was wrong, just not that this much was wrong.

Dionne looked terrified. She hung back at the far end of the room, near the kitchen. "Would you like a cup of tea?"

She tried to make it sound as if this was perfectly normal. As if most people lived in empty houses. He wondered if she even had a kettle to boil water. He looked up uncertainly at her. "Dionne," he started. "Do you have some kind of drug problem?"

"Drugs?" Her eyes widened, and for a moment she relaxed, laughing at the ridiculousness of the suggestion. "Jesus, no; I can't afford drugs."

"But it looks like you've sold all your gear."

She swallowed at the air. Where to even begin? "I don't really know where to start." They both looked down at the neat piles of face-down papers lined up in the middle of the room. She had not told anyone about this. She walked over to the shelf, picking up a couple of pieces of rose quartz as a distraction and nervously shook them around in her hand. "I'm broke."

"You're broke?"

There was the understatement of the year. She looked at the floor. "I owe money."

So this was why she had panicked and walked out. Thinking back over the little signs – waiting for a free lift to York; telling her father she was in between phones (she had just cancelled the landline because of the expense); always on the look out for free food; working herself to death six days a week. He was starting to wonder himself just what kind of a mess he'd walked in on. He looked uncertainly over at her. "You don't mean loan sharks?"

"Oh no," she assured him. "I only have debts with reputable companies: banks and credit cards."

As if that was a mere trifle.

"If it's not prying, can I ask how much you owe?"

"Give or take?"

He nodded, not sure he wanted to know. "Give or take."

She shrugged and looked out the window. As if she didn't know. She knew those debts down to the last penny. Very exact and demanding close friends that would not go away until they'd been satisfied. She didn't like saying the amount out loud. It reminded her that it was real. Give or take. "About fifty," she paused, catching his eye. He was vainly hoping she was going to say fifty quid. "About fifty thousand pounds."

He looked visibly shaken. If this was a mortgage they were talking about, he could understand it. But she was renting. Bricks and mortar were not involved. "Jesus, Dionne," he broke out. "How the hell did you get to the stage of owing fifty grand?"

"I didn't have any choice."

"And how long has this been going on?"

"The last two years."

That was a long time to be stressed under this amount of debt. Two years of working to the bone. And she was probably barely even meeting the interest if a lot of credit cards were involved. She obviously didn't spend any money – certainly not on her home. Her life was bare essentials and work. But what kind of a life was that? He watched her standing at the side of the room. Thin and nervous. Her hands were shaking.

"You need to apply for bankruptcy."

"No." Her voice was sharp and definite on this issue. No compromise. "Besides, I don't suppose I could afford it even if it were an option. You know it costs money to apply for bankruptcy?"

"But you can't go on like this. I can't imagine you're earning big wages at the bookshop or the pub. If you owe money on credit cards, it'll take you forever to pay them off. The only other way I can see you saving money is on your rent, but you have to live somewhere."

"I did look at bedsits once," she admitted. "But it was just too depressing and there was little privacy. I just couldn't face it. I suppose the only other alternative is quitting my jobs here and moving in with Dad. But then I'd have to tell him."

"He doesn't know?"

She shook her head.

It probably was the best option if she was determined to pay it all back, because she needed to up her available cash, but he didn't want to think about her moving away. "How did you get to the point of owing fifty grand?"

"Maggie died," she said simply, leaning against the wall. She had thought this would be worse than it was. Actually, it was quite a relief to be able to explain herself to someone. Hope that she would get a pat on the head at the end and be told that anyone could have ended up in this mess. "Maggie was my father's partner and she died. They were never married. They lived together in the house at York and it completely devastated my father when she died. He couldn't cope with anything. I had to help him with a lot. I think if he'd had to leave the house, he would have fallen apart for good.

"She'd made a will just before she died. She left the house to my father, split her money between her relatives." She paused, looking at Jack. "People are greedy. Wills seem to bring out the worst in people. Her family contested the will, said they should have the house as well. Maggie had never married my father, he was just *some* boyfriend, they said.

"The court found in their favour and gave them a part share in the house. My father had to buy them out. He was a mental wreck. I helped him out with some money. Oh, it was money I had. The last of my money."

"So where did the fifty grand come from?"

"Some of that is interest." She sat down on the floor beside her bank and credit card statements. All in the red. "Filippo got himself a new wife and she wanted the money back. I had to pay it all back immediately. I'd just given the last of it to my father for the house."

"Who's Filippo?"

"Filippo is an Italian man I lived with for about a year. In Rome. I went there as a student to study the language. I was only supposed to be there six months before going to Iceland."

"Iceland?" Her life was growing more complicated by the second. His life seemed rather dull and mediocre in comparison. He didn't have any secrets like this to share with her.

"I did a joint honours degree at university in Italian and Icelandic," she quickly explained. "Shortly after I'd moved to Rome, I met Filippo. I was only twenty when I went there and he was a few years older. Treated me like a princess." She shook her head in disgust at herself. "I moved in with him a couple of months after meeting him. Dropped out of uni, stopped doing anything much at all. I just stayed in his flat and ate and spent all my money."

"So this Filippo gave you some money to help you get going again."

The way he said Filippo's name made it clear he didn't like the man. They'd never even met and Filippo had never really done anything wrong. Men and their territorial rights. Dionne shook her head. "No. I hacked into his account and transferred money into my account. Thirty thousand or so." Give or take. Although with the exchange rates it had been nearer forty thousand. She couldn't look at Jack. It was done now. She was a thief. It was admitted. The woman who had lived off men. A parasite. He wasn't going to want her now.

She had to finish her story. "I had to get back to the UK and sort myself out. I wanted to finish my degree. I was studying in London, and everything was so expensive. I was terrified Filippo would come after me. I needed to hide so I said I would study in Reykjavik for a year. Iceland isn't cheap either. I thought he couldn't find me, but he told me that he had always known where I was. He was prepared to let me get away with it."

"He must have really loved you."

"I don't know whether love was ever really the word with Filippo. Anyway, then he got married, his wife found out what had happened and demanded the money be paid back immediately. She threatened legal action, but Filippo managed to negotiate. If I paid it all back straight away, the police would never know. So I borrowed the money and paid him back.

"So there you have it. I am completely broke and I owe thousands. And I am not some innocent little victim hit hard by circumstance. I stole that money. And this is why I have to be on my own. Who is going to trust me? Besides, it will take me decades to pay off all my debts. Decades of living and working like this."

"Declare bankruptcy."

"And let other people pay off my mistakes?" She looked him in the eye for the first time since she had begun her story. "How is that fair? I have to take the consequences of my actions."

Jack was bowled over. This he had not expected.

"I try not to think about it too much, the full amount," she continued. She was babbling now, nervous. Terrified of the silence. Of what he might tell her. "I feel ill at night thinking about it. I sometimes get panic attacks, just wondering how on earth I am going to get this all paid back." She stopped chattering as she felt his fingers on the side of her face.

"I think that's enough confession for one day." He had knelt down beside her. He'd have to let all of this sink in, let his brain sort it out. No more talk of money tonight. "Now, do you still have a bed in this place, or did you sell that as well?"

She shook her head. "I kept the bed. It's through there."

She looked shattered. He picked her up. "I think you need to get some sleep," he told her.

The Professor Hammond Wagstaff lived in a reasonably large, comfortable two storey house in a small cul-de-sac on the edge of town. His front room was like a library; tall glass-panelled bookcases containing volumes on the weather lining the walls. The weather collection: decades' worth of collecting from academia across the globe. It was something the Professor was particularly proud of.

The usually calm, thoughtful atmosphere in his living room – personally the Professor preferred to refer to the room as his study (as if he lived in an old mansion) – was lost. They were quiet and tense. Words unspoken. He didn't know what the problem was but they should have been more talkative than this.

It was a couple of weeks since Dionne's particularly moody day. She had settled down, become distinctly brighter and even allowed another member into the society, all in advance of today's Sunday afternoon meeting. Usually she was full of ideas, excited to investigate the details behind the stories, but she had arrived and slumped into the armchair. She looked exhausted. Still working six days a week at the bookshop, still working at the pub. But there was something else.

He was surprised to say it himself, but the something else seemed to be Alan. The Professor had half expected Alan not to come. No one had really seen Alan since the assault several weeks ago. The bruises had gone down, the physical damage healed, but Alan stayed at home and didn't go out. From what the Professor heard from the mother, he wasn't looking for a new job since quitting at the quarry. He wasn't doing anything, just sitting up in his room. He wasn't interested in continuing with the reading lessons either. No one seemed to be able to get through to him.

The Professor had rung and left a message to let him know they were having another meeting of the Society of Lost Causes. He hadn't expected Alan to come, so it had been a surprise when Alan was the first to arrive. Barely said a word, came in and sat in a hard-backed chair at the rear of the room. As if he was observing but didn't really want to join in.

Jack was going to get a very wrong impression of their little association from this meeting.

"Well," the Professor clapped his hands together, his voice louder than usual. "Shall we start on our discussions? One thing I think we need to consider is that we haven't made any future plans."

Dionne jumped as the notepad resting on her lap slipped to the floor. "What do you mean?" she asked as she leaned forward to pick it up.

"Jonathan Martin has a couple more weeks to go, then we'll be putting up Saskia Weaver and associates. Beyond that we have no subjects up for consideration. We haven't started on anything. I don't know what to plan for the shop."

"You're wanting something new to investigate?" Jack, sat in the armchair directly opposite Dionne, looked over at the Professor.

"Exactly."

"How about the Devil's Arrows?"

"As opposed to cupid's?" the Professor asked slyly.

Dionne rolled her eyes. The Professor had been worse than a middle aged housewife for gossip and innuendo the last couple of weeks, hinting and digging that there might be something between her and Jack. Of course, the more he niggled, the more inclined she felt like stringing it out. Besides, they didn't need to make a big deal out of the fact that she was tentatively starting a relationship. Didn't want to jinx it. Dionne told herself it was just the beginning. Jack seemed to be settled on the forever after already. Your problems are my problems. He came up with suggestions to help her pay back her debts more quickly, most of them revolving around a theme of her quitting her flat and moving in with him. She told him she didn't want to become that dependant on a man again. Jack nodded and smiled and changed the subject for a couple of days.

"As in megalithic monuments," Dionne corrected the Professor, well-aware he already knew what they were talking about. "Over at Boroughbridge."

"Oh, those," the Professor said as if the thought had never occurred to him.

Jack was staring at Dionne. Remembering Boroughbridge. The trip to York.

"I thought it would be good if we brought in some other subjects in besides purely focusing on the biographies of the lost souls of history," Hammond suggested. "I was thinking something to do with cloud formations. An introduction to get us going."

"Maybe we could have a competition at the shop," Dionne added. "A photography competition of weird cloud shapes."

"That would be good," the Professor agreed, thinking of his archives of personal photographs. He could win such a competition hands down. Being the proprietor he probably shouldn't enter.

"Do you think I'll be a lost soul of history?"

They had forgotten Alan was in the room. They looked to the back of the library, where Alan sat upright, his hands gripping the arms of the chair. He didn't look overly happy.

The Professor didn't understand exactly what he meant. "I'm sorry, Alan?"

"The man who got the shit kicked out of him. The man wrongly accused of Trevor Washington's murder. I must count as a lost cause."

Hammond laughed awkwardly. "You are hardly a lost cause."

"I'm an unknown, insignificant type that Dionne likes to pin up on her board," Alan continued, glaring at the only woman in the room with distinct bitterness. "Interesting anecdotes to laugh about at the pub."

Dionne felt mildly sick. Alan looked furious, as if she had personally attacked him. She hadn't done anything to hurt Alan. She hoped this wasn't because she had accidentally walked in on him when he had been crying in the back room. She hadn't meant to intrude. She had only meant well. "Alan, I..."

"I think you forget that these were real people. They really suffered. For them, it was awful."

"I haven't forgotten they were real. The whole point is to stop them being forgotten."

"Like Saskia Weaver," he leaned forward. He looked like a mangy spiteful cat just out of the rain. "You'll be pinning her back up in the public glare soon."

"She is the next..."

"Did you all hear that they caught that bloke's killer last night?"

The loud and abrupt question silenced everyone. A change of subject. Purposefully timed. No more hypotheses in the village. No more suggestions and wild accusations. No more beatings of innocent men. Only one to lynch now. Judging by the lack of response, no one else had heard the news.

Alan was ready to explode. The Professor felt they needed to tread carefully around this one. "We haven't heard, Alan."

"Oh yes," Alan confirmed, looking directly at Dionne. As if he would jump up and explain why they were all gathered here today. He had been investigating the crime, and had realised someone present in the room today had committed the murder. "They went to arrest him last night. He confessed straight away. Bit of a headcase; doesn't understand guilt. He'd only recently been let out of a nuthouse. They caught him with a library ticket."

Alan paused on this random revelation and no one bothered to ask questions. They could tell Alan wanted to tell this story; he would not be quiet until he had said what he had to say. He'd never had so much to say all at once. Never been this articulate. It was as if he had spent these weeks locked in his room planning this outburst. Carefully crafting every sentence. Dionne's fingers were tight around the edges of her hardback note pad. She didn't know this story, but judging from Alan's expression, there was something bad coming.

"He lives in Northallerton. Couldn't get a job, so he spent a lot of time wandering. Went to the library a lot. Found a book left out on a table because *someone* couldn't be bothered with putting it away. It was a local history book. There was a section about Saskia Weaver in it. The police say he related to her suffering."

Dionne stared at the floor.

"Said he got a bit obsessed with her. Was convinced they were soul mates."

She felt nauseous.

"He came up to our little town to see the place where she'd died. Went up to the folly. He thinks she was buried there. Thought she'd return from the dead to be with him. He told the police that she was starting to materialise in front of him." Alan paused, looking around the room. "Then some idiot rolled up and started taking photographs."

The silence was choking. The Professor coughed. "How do you know all this?"

"Bumped into Seger this morning. So you see, it all goes back to this book. If *someone* hadn't forgotten to put the book back on the shelf, he would never have come here. He would never have bumped into Trevor Washington and slit his throat."

"If he was a headcase, someone was going to get on the wrong side of him sooner or later," Jack spoke. "You can't put the blame for something like that on anyone but the headcase."

Alan was up on his feet. "I got the living shit kicked out of me because of him. They called me a freak and said I liked killing people. I didn't do nothing!" he screamed, shaking his fists at Dionne. "It's all your fault. Reading about your stupid stories about stupid dead people as if anyone gives a shit…"

"Alan, you need to calm down," the Professor said strictly.

"Because she hasn't got a life of her own she has to mess about with stuff like that and get people killed." He made a move as if to attack Dionne, but thought better of it when he saw how quickly Jack moved up from his seat. No one was moving to hit him because they all pitied him. Thought he was a stupid lad, a child, and he wasn't worth it. Those drunken thugs hadn't thought so. He didn't need their pity. "I've had it with you lot. With this fucking town," he announced loudly. "My uncle's got me a job in Harrogate. You won't see me round here again. You lot can rot in your own hell." He glowered at Dionne before running out of the building. If it hadn't been so serious, the flouncing manner of his sprint would have almost seemed comical.

Jack moved towards her.

"Don't," she said sharply, jumping to her feet. Her fingers were vacuumed around the notepad. Clinging on for life.

"You can't take anything he just said to heart."

"I want to be on my own for a while," she said, moving for the exit.

"Dionne…"

"No!" She marched out of the building, clutching the book to her chest, determined not to cry.

The Professor watched her go from the window. "She probably needs a bit of space right now," he advised Jack.

"She doesn't need this at the moment."

"I don't suppose any of us do," the Professor murmured. He paused, moving away from his own problems to examine Jack. Did he know what it was that haunted Dionne? "We've got to remember that no one is responsible for the murder apart from the man who committed it."

"I know."

"We've got to make sure she understands it."

Everything became more vivid in the rain. The dark rocks in the mortar of the wall. The plants, the trees, the undergrowth, the patterns in the tree bark, the lines of water running across her skin, the dirt where the grass had been scraped away, the dark marks that might be the remnants of blood splatter.

Dionne clutched at the wall of the folly and gasped. The rain water ran down her back, binding her hair into rags. Her eyes were so full of tears and rainwater that she couldn't focus on anything. She scrabbled at the book of notes, tearing out pages and yelling at herself, shredding the paper, throwing soggy scraps at nothing.

She craned her neck back and sobbed at the sky. The clouds pulled in together and looked back down in judgement.

Is this all her pathetic existence amounted to?

The side of the folly was rough under the palms of her hands, but she clung on, cursing the name of Saskia Weaver. That she had ever come across the name and thought it would be fun to read up on. That she hadn't reshelved that book. That Trevor Washington had ever come here.

If only they had never been stupid enough to believe Saskia Weaver was a witch. None of this would ever have happened.

People jeered and screamed. Contorted faces, red angry skin, vicious, eyes narrowed in fury. So much hatred. So much misunderstanding. The stench was almost unbearable. Unwashed bodies, rotten fruit, manure, and somewhere in the distance, the scent of smoke. Her stomach turned as she realised what it was to be.

Sunlight pinched at the backs of her eyes as she was brought from her cell. People grabbed at her, tearing her clothes. Taking fistfuls of her long mahogany, flame-tinged locks and pulling her head this way and that. She cried out in pain.

After everything that had happened to her, it was to end like this. Not end, it would never end. But she couldn't see a way out and she feared the pain. People were screaming for blood. Burn her! Burn, burn! She had never done anything wrong to hurt this community.

Her jailors dragged her exhausted frame up the cobbles towards the place of execution. The bonfire. Piled high with extra faggots. She could see the men standing with torches. She screamed out for mercy. People spat in her face; the body-warm, thick saliva running down the side of her face and splattering to the ground. Someone lobbed rotten fruit at her. Women ran forward and scratched at her face. Mass hysteria. It wouldn't solve a single one of their problems.

Up at the end of the march of death, in the heaving crowds, she spotted Andrew Holburn. Her supporter. He had always defended her case. Begged people for science and reason. For logic. He wouldn't look her in the eye now.

"Holburn," she called out to him as they approached, straining against the thick arms of the jailors. "You have to help me."

The pitiful wretch. He had never seen anyone as terrified as her. Her hair torn and tangled, her clothes like rags. Red scratches on her skin. Dirt, smears, spittle. He lowered his eyes away from her. "There's nothing I can do," he whispered.

"Mr Holburn, you've always helped me. You have to save me."

It took all his courage to look her in the eye. "I've seen what you can do."

Oh no, not him as well, no, no, no. "You don't understand."

The men pulled her back. They wanted her dead. No more conversation. No more plans from Mr Holburn to try and save her. Everyone knew she was a witch. She had to die.

Saskia broke free for a moment, lurching forward to grab onto the neat velvet sleeve of Mr Holburn's jacket. She was desperate. She would do anything. Anything but death she could do. "Please, you don't understand." She tugged at his arm. "They can't kill me."

Andrew Holburn looked at her wide, fearful eyes. "There is nothing I can do."

Someone grabbed at the back of her dress, tearing the material and revealing her shoulder. People screamed when they saw a part of the tattoo, like black flames creeping up her skin. This one was marked for the fire.

"The brand of the devil!" someone in the crowd shouted.

Saskia Weaver was dragged up the pile of fagots like a bundle of rags and tied securely to the stake. The crowds backed far enough away for their own safety, but remained to watch; jeering and screaming. The fires were lit. Saskia joined in the screaming as her skirts caught alight, the heat rising up her flesh. The smoke twisted in her lungs. Her cries were worse than anything they had heard, from death, accident or childbirth. She writhed and tried in vain to break from her bonds. She screamed and screamed. The flames licked higher and set her hair alight. Her flesh began to roast on her bones, her skin angry red and peeling. Her scalded head. She stared out at Andrew Holburn, still desperate for rescue. He couldn't watch this. Stony faced, he turned and walked away from the scene.

Even when her eyes burst from the heat and ran down her disintegrating cheeks she did not loose consciousness. She screamed in agony. A hush fell upon the crowd. People felt ill. Many had to leave. They said she didn't loose consciousness when others usually did because of the red in her hair. Because she felt more. Because she was a witch, and God had picked her out to suffer. Because she was evil.

Her head slumped forward, her body barely visible through the fierce flames. People could still hear her screams, not sure if it was in their memory or the sound was still echoing throughout the town.

The fire burned through the night. In the morning there was a smouldering clump of heavy ashes. The remains of Saskia Weaver were there if you cared to pick through the charred masses.

The scent of burned human flesh was in the air. Miles away in his family home, Andrew Holburn sat locked in his study and grieved. Convinced she had been a witch by something he had seen that no one had brought to the trial. Something he had never told a living soul. He could still hear her screaming. Even now. Would she never rest?

He closed his eyes and remembered her terrified look. The desperation. 'They can't kill me'. Her words echoed around him. He wondered if they had all misunderstood exactly what she had meant by that. Perhaps there was a reason he was sure he could still hear her screams. Faint and distant now, but she was still suffering. Maybe forever.

The sound of flames roaring was all consuming. The woman screamed in agony as she was burned alive. Harrowing to watch, but she couldn't look away. She simply could not stop herself.

There was a man running through the crowds to the bonfire, a burning torch held aloft. He threw it into the flames, and there was a boom, like an explosion as the fire suddenly grew in size. Everyone stumbled back in panic, fearful they would get caught up in the inferno.

Dionne's eyes were wide open. It was dark. Sometime in the early morning. So silent. The world was sleeping. The sound of the explosion continued to reverberate through the room. It had been a particularly lucid nightmare. She'd been dreaming about Saskia Weaver a lot the last month, ever since Alan had screamed at them in the Professor's house and stormed out. They had not seen him since. The Professor had heard from Alan's mother that he was now living in Harrogate.

She sat up in bed. She felt too alert, too unsettled to drift back into sleep. There was something about that particular dream that made it worse than the others. Something was not quite right. She shivered, pulling on the sleeves of her pyjama top, and glanced across at the digital clock. Half past two in the morning.

Jack rolled over in bed and mumbled something. Dionne looked down at him. "Are you awake?" she whispered.

"Hmmm."

"Did you just hear a big bang?"

"No," he sighed, slinging a sleep heavy arm around the front of her waist.

"I can't sleep," she said. "I'm going downstairs to get some water."

Bare foot, Dionne padded downstairs to the kitchen. The electric light seemed hollow and dulled. She took a glass from the cupboard, filled it with water, and sat down at the table. She was still renting her little empty home, but was spending increasingly more time sleeping over at Jack's. It was warmer here, happier, distanced from all her woes and stresses. And although independence was always an essential asset for long-living, company was incredibly pleasurable.

She sipped the water and pondered on the Saskia Weaver display. It would have to be done – they had nothing else ready to replace Jonathan Martin. Despite the fact that she had destroyed most of her notes and didn't want to discuss the subject, she remembered enough to put something half decent together. Suggested reading lists had been drawn up and Hammond had said they should go through the final list tomorrow – no, today it was now – and get the books ordered.

She downed the rest of the water and went back to the warm bed.

A few hours later Dionne was walking to work. She followed her new route to work – from Jack's house – and unlocked the bookshop doors and let herself in. Switched off the alarm and wandered through to the back room to put the kettle on. Hammond wasn't in yet, but recently he'd been getting later and later in arriving. He had things on his mind. Hadn't mentioned anything to Dionne, but she supposed he would tell her when and if he ever felt ready. She didn't have any right to ask.

She switched on the computer and checked the morning's emails. Nothing interesting. Went through and switched on the lights in the bookshelves. Tidied round and removed a couple of dead flies from the front windowsill.

At half past nine, P.C Sam Seger entered the bookshop. At that precise moment Amanda was telling Jack the news she had just picked up from Terry the postman. Jack was so shocked he threw his tea down his T-shirt. Dionne was stood at the cash till. Her heart had sank when she had seen Seger, and she had been ready to throw him out. For all his irritations, Seger could be effective at his job, and forwarded the news quickly and to the point. There was no easy way to deal with this kind of task. Best to get the facts out as soon as possible. Dionne's knees buckled and she dropped out of sight behind the desk.

Seger crept forward, always a little apprehensive of Dionne, even now. She was crumbled on the floor, staring at the carpet as if it didn't make sense.

"Dionne? Are you all right? Can you speak to me?"

She looked up at him blankly. A moment of nothing. Then her eyes narrowed. She pulled herself back up. "Get out of here."

"Dionne…"

"Out." She pointed at the door. "I don't need to listen to your rubbish."

She did look disturbingly pale. It was an old cliché, but he had literally seen the colour fall out of her face as he had told her. Then she had lost control over her limbs. Was this shock? Probably, and no doubt it was going to get worse. "I'll get the doctor," he told her.

"I don't need a doctor," Dionne scoffed.

He shouldn't be leaving her alone, but Dionne was resolute he left the building. As Seger stepped out of the bookshop he saw Jack Dougan, the cinema projectionist marching up the high street. He had a large dark stain down the front of his T-shirt. Seger had heard that Dionne and Dougan had something going on.

"Have you told her?" Jack asked as he approached the bookshop.

Seger nodded grimly. "I presume you've heard on the grapevine." Nothing got around as quickly as bad news. He was a little surprised that she hadn't known when he had arrived. "I'm going to get the doctor," Seger told him. "I think she's going into shock."

"Do that." Jack shut the door in his face.

Inside Dionne was scrabbling at papers on the desk as if she had just lost her passport and needed to board a flight. She glanced up as Jack walked into the shop. "I've lost my lists," she told him as she continued to search. She made it sound like she was talking about her mind. "We're finalising our order for the month today and I've lost my lists."

"They can wait." Jack walked up to the desk. He took her hands and set them firmly down. Just stop. No more worrying, no rushing around. Dionne slowly looked up at him. "I think the order can wait a few days, don't you?"

"We need…" Dionne started.

He shushed her, putting a finger to her lips.

"Hammond's going to…" She looked away and couldn't finish the sentence.

Jack took her through to the back room and set her down on the settee. He went through the shop and turned off the lights. Set the sign to closed and turned the latch on the door. He finished making the tea and gave her a cup.

Dionne sat on the end of the settee, hunched up and silent, staring at the cupboard door. She didn't say a word. There were tears in her eyes. She turned to him, opened her mouth to say something, but she'd lost the ability to speak. She gagged on her words and started to cry. Started to shake. It felt as though the world was crumbling down upon her.

Sounds became dull, as if she were swimming underwater, everyone else high up there on dry land, talking about something, giving her concerned looks. The doctor had arrived at some point. She could see Seger in the back ground. The doctor was talking to Jack, passing him a piece of paper, telling him to go to the chemist and home. Dionne wanted to ask what was the matter with Jack, but she felt as though she was having trouble breathing. There was too much water in her eyes.

She sat meekly as the computer was switched off. They all left the building. Jack locked up and took her home. Leading her like a mindless child. There was something shouting in her head, but Dionne didn't want to listen. She didn't want to be here at all.

The Professor Hammond Wagstaff's funeral service was held on a Wednesday morning at the little wind-blown churchyard over looking the town and the Dales. It was a particularly cloudy day and the Professor would have approved of the cloud formations. It was as if his old friends had rolled up to pay their last respects.

A small gathering stood in the graveyard where the memorial stone had been placed. The wind rippled through skirts and long coats, hair that wasn't carefully pinned down in place. It danced through the flowers in the wreaths, ruffled through the pages of the book the vicar was trying to read. The Professor had never struck him as a religious man, but no one had been sure what to do, so he had stepped in and offered his services.

Dionne Nelson, in a long black dress, hung on the arm of Jack Dougan as if unable to support her own weight. Her other hand rested limply on the corner of her father's arm. Surrounding them were a sombre collection of academic professors and doctors, neighbouring businessmen and women from the high street. Friends and well wishers. No family. As far as anyone knew, the Professor did not have any living relations. Mark Grierson, Charlotta and a few other regulars from the pub, stood on the sidelines. They hadn't really known the Professor all that well, but turned up in solidarity for Dionne. Sam Seger loitered in the background, thinking of every occasion he and the Professor had met and wound one another up the wrong way. At the far end of the group, Alan stood in a borrowed suit, suddenly aged with the shock of the news. He hadn't dared speak to Dionne or Jack since arriving, and had hidden himself away at the edge of the group, almost embarrassed to be present.

At 2.30am on the previous Tuesday morning, the Professor's house had exploded. The report from fire service stated that it had been a gas leak. The fire had been particularly fierce and fast, and had incinerated most of the contents. The explosion originated in the kitchen, where the Professor's charred remains had been gathered. It was general opinion that the man would have been killed instantaneously. Be grateful for small mercies.

The remains were collected, and as if an ironic wink to his death, he was cremated – the crematorium's furnace finishing what the local firemen had not allowed the house fire to do. The ashes were now in a small black urn waiting to be scattered when Dionne felt ready for the task.

Dionne barely registered what the vicar was saying. She still felt as though someone had sliced out a chunk of her innards. She didn't have many friends and allies in this world. The Professor may have been her employer, but they had had a close bond, and she felt lost without it. Her whole world now stood on either side of her.

As the vicar drew to a close, she glanced up and saw Alan. He looked devastated, as well he should considering how much help the Professor had given him. Hammond had been upset when Alan had furiously marched out of their lives, although he had tried his best not to show it. As far as Dionne knew, the two never spoke again after that awful day.

The vicar closed his book. People lingered for a moment, realising this was it. They would not see that eccentric, long haired bookseller in town again, gazing at the skies and smiling to himself. The gathering started to disperse. People ambled slowly down the hillside, back in to town towards the pub.

A short man in a grey suit, glasses and grey hair, hurried up to Alan and tapped him respectfully on the shoulder. They exchanged a few words, Alan nodded solemnly and went down the hill. The little man remained, looking over the crowds and focusing on Dionne.

"Dionne Nelson?" he asked as he cautiously approached. "Please accept my apologies for the intrusion at this time. And my condolences for this tragedy."

Dionne smiled weakly at him, purely for his benefit.

"My name is Howard Jones."

"It's nice to meet you Mr Jones. I'm sorry, I don't remember the Professor ever mentioning you," she said quietly. She didn't want to have those conversations right now. What a marvellous man he had been. What a character. A loss to the community.

"I'm not surprised really," he told her. "I was the Professor Wagstaff's solicitor. I am sorry for the urgency in this matter, but I need to speak to you and Alan Marks together, and my understanding is that Mr Marks now lives in Harrogate. I also appreciate that we need to discuss matters as I believe you are temporarily running the shop on your own until the future of the Professor's assets have been finalised."

Dionne felt sick. She was going to get thrown out of the bookshop now. It would close. Of course she couldn't continue with things as they had been.

"Could you spare me half an hour?" the solicitor asked. "I've asked Mr Marks to join us down at the bookshop. I thought it would be a good place to gather. I won't keep you too long so that you can join the others."

Graham Nelson looked down at his daughter with sadness. He knew all too well how grief was. "Do you want us to go with you?"

She surprised both her father and Jack with her answer. "No." she said. "I'll be fine. I'll see you at the pub."

She had to deal with this death and she had to take what ever further knocks were coming to her standing up. She was going to have a lot of tough choices to make in the near future and she needed to be strong.

Dionne and Mr Jones walked down to the bookshop. Alan was waiting outside, looking fearful. He hadn't been in the town since that day he had cut himself off from the society. He looked sadly at Dionne. "I'm really sorry about what I said."

She shook her head. "It doesn't matter."

Howard Jones waited until they were both settled on the settees in the bookshop before he started to explain why he needed to see them just now. "This is just a preliminary, you understand," he said as he sat down on the settee next to Alan. "I'm not sure if you're both aware, but the Professor Wagstaff had no living relatives. This isn't meant to be a formal reading of the will, but I need to get in touch with the beneficiaries to let them know. There were some bequests to academic institutions as well – I won't take up your time with the details today."

The little man paused to take some papers out of his briefcase. "Firstly, the Professor had a particularly large collection of books on meteorology."

Dionne flicked her gaze out of the window. This was making her feel ill. The man had only been dead a week, and it was business as usual, picking over the remains, sorting out the material wealth.

"The Professor left the entire collection to you, Mr Marks."

Both Dionne and Alan looked in surprise at the solicitor. He'd left his precious collection of books to Alan? Dionne couldn't help herself, if the Professor was going to leave her anything, she would have thought he might have mentioned a book. Suddenly feeling tired, she pressed a couple of fingers at the centre of her brow. "He kept his books at the house. They went up in flames."

"Some did," the solicitor agreed. "And you will get the monetary value from the house insurance for those destroyed books when it has been processed," he told Alan. "However, it has come to my attention that the Professor actually lent a great number of those books to an old colleague now working at York University. I've spoken to the gentleman in question, and he says he can get the books to you as soon as you want them. He doesn't have any particular need of them."

"I don't deserve this," Alan spoke quietly. "I shouted at him. That's the last thing I did."

Dionne looked at the floor. There wasn't much they could do to change the past.

"I'm sure he understands that it was just the heat of the moment," the solicitor said.

Alan was as white as bleached paper. He shook his head. "I don't feel well. I need to get some air." He got up and walked out the door, pacing on the pavement on the high street.

"Miss Nelson."

Dionne looked blankly at Mr Jones.

"We need to discuss the bookshop."

She sighed. "I know. What's going to happen to it? Is it going to be sold as a going concern?"

"That depends on the new owner."

"Do you think I'll keep my job?"

He smiled sympathetically at her. "I don't think you quite understand. The Professor owned this building. It isn't rented. The building, the stock, the business, they all come as a whole."

"I know he owns this building. He always said it was good he didn't have a landlord to bother with."

"He left the business to you."

She didn't know what to say. What to think. "What do you mean...?"

"You are the sole benefactor of the business. You now own the entire business... well, after probate has gone through of course."

It was too much. She didn't deserve any of this. She wished Hammond wasn't dead, but surely, in the awful circumstances, someone else, something else had to be more deserving.

"What you do with the business is of course, up to you," he continued, flicking through his papers. "Apart from the business, you were also left the house. The insurance payout, minus the value of the destroyed books left to Mr Marks, will go to you. I believe there was a life insurance policy as well, which will go to you. There are a few accounts, but these have been left to various academic institutions."

Dionne covered her eyes with her hands. She felt terrible.

"I understand you didn't realise any of this had been arranged?"

She shook her head.

"I appreciate this is a lot to take in, especially at this time. It will seem like a large burden, but please don't worry. This won't be immediate; probate does have to go through. And from the insurances you will be left with a large disposable income so you have no need to worry about the death duties."

She squeezed her eyes shut, even though they were covered by her hands.

"All in all, Miss Nelson," the solicitor concluded. "You have just become a rather wealthy woman."

One year later

Dionne locked the door to the bookshop and turned to face the quiet rows of books. It had been a while since she had worked a full day on her own in the shop. She went to sit down on one of the settees and thought about Hammond. It was just past the year since he had died. Killed by the gas explosion. Nasty accidents at home.

It had been hard getting used to the new life, and at times she had found it virtually impossible getting out of bed on a morning. She had come to depend on a few familiar faces in her life; her rocks, her steadfasts. He was gone. One of her best friends, if she was honest, and she still missed him even now.

Mr Jones, the solicitor had been a great help at the beginning. Arrangements had been made so that she had enough temporary financial control to look after the business. Suddenly her work had mushroomed. She'd had to take on a woman part time to help her. Dionne had been exhausted, and had had to quit the shifts at the pub. Of course, when the final amounts were agreed, she knew she would have enough to pay the inheritance tax and clear her own personal debts, but in the interim before the transfer of funds was complete, she had needed money to try and keep up with repayments. She handed in her notice for her empty little flat, packed up the few remaining belongings she still had, and moved in with Jack.

Dionne stretched back in the settee and put her feet up on the table. A lot had changed in the past year. A sleepy town where things never seemed to change. The last few months had been a whirlwind for everyone.

Jack's colleague from the periodical returned from his longship adventure and took over the reigns of the magazine. Jack was still a sub editor and contributed articles, but the sheer number of hours of devotion dropped. The timing coincided with the changes at the cinema. He had taken a couple of months to train up a new projectionist at the cinema, then dropped down to being a reserve projectionist because of other events.

Amanda Turner resigned from the cinema shortly after the Professor's death, neither event connected. She took a job with the Yorkshire Arts Council and moved down to Leeds. Jack said he'd look after the cinema on a temporary basis until a replacement was found, but as yet he still hadn't bothered to pen the job advertisement.

Dionne now looked after a staff of two at the bookshop – one part timer and one full timer. She didn't know how she and the Professor had managed as they had for those three years.

She was gradually making changes. The upstairs floor was renovated and tidied out. She had two rooms for the second hand book business to run from, in peace away from the main shop. She had made a staffroom upstairs as well, because she couldn't endure to be in the back room of the shop. It had taken months before she had dared to go and clear out the Professor's desk. Collections of old delivery notes, doodles, indecipherable scrawl, receipts, postcards from friends, photographs of cloud formations, a few boiled sweets in plastic wrappers, articles about tribes in South America and jewels from the Middle East torn out of magazines, newspaper articles and a printout from the internet on brain tumours. She had scrumpled up the sheets and thrown them in the corner. Thought about how good luck had it that his favourite books had been sent to York two weeks before the explosion. How Hammond joked that his rickety old gas heating system would be the death of him. Especially that gas hob top you had to light with matches.

Of course, it was just as likely that it had been an accident, for there was nothing stranger that truth. Coincidences never ceased to amaze.

Dionne had picked up the crumpled papers and her bag before retreating to the bathroom. Putting down the lid, she sat on the toilet and smoothed out the papers on her bag. Looked over the ethereal images of brain scans. It could just as easily have been a random passing curiosity. Nothing more, nothing less. She didn't know.

She cried for the loss of her friend. Then she put up the toilet lid and took the test she'd been carrying in her bag for the last week, and cried a little more when she discovered she was indeed pregnant.

The Society of Lost Causes never formally met again. The line of displays in the bookshop ended with the name of Saskia Weaver. Alan sporadically kept in touch, but he never did know quite what to say. Without the Professor, it didn't seem right. Dionne had set up the society, but she supposed it had really been Hammond that had held it all together. You couldn't kill the curiosity they all had for life, but it went back to being a private, personal pastime.

The Professor's ashes were scattered on a field after the landowner's permission had been granted. A field on the steep banks of the hills, a view point down the Dales. The sun light cut through the clouds, and Dionne had thrown the ashes up into the air. The wind picked them up and took them away to take part in the weather patterns across the world. Somewhere in town, she liked a think a few specks of Hammond Wagstaff danced with a few specks of Saskia Weaver and remembered that there was always something left to smile about.

Even when it did seem like a lost cause.

Lovers of Old Films
Ophelia Finsen

Fresh from university and eager for the rest of his life, Edward Gable moves to York to start a position in a graduate training scheme. And whilst real life may not meet his expectations, the building he moves into can more than compensate for the lack of excitement. Certainly everyone is friendly and helpful, but there are secrets no one wants to talk about – and if you find yourself living in a building with Sophia Loren, you know something out of the ordinary is going to happen.

Ever wanted to be your idol?
You might want to think again...